B S M E L M B P J R O P S

O W P E O R N C   P9-EMH-458

T H L O V E V M E L M F

O R I S N A B Z V X F Q Z

S L D I S H O N O R Y V C

I A O W P E O R N N T H E

B G P R M A R R Y W P E C

U R N J T L P F Q H N

E F W B M E L M D I E M

N A B N M T O P S Z X Z T

M I S C H E R I S H F A I

O F P R G L D O I B B Y E I D

N P P E R I S H E L M L P

B S M E L M B P O R O P S

A I V L M A G N O V E L R L

O R I S N A B Z V F O Z

ALSO BY DAVID RAKOFF

Half Empty
Don't Get Too Comfortable
Fraud

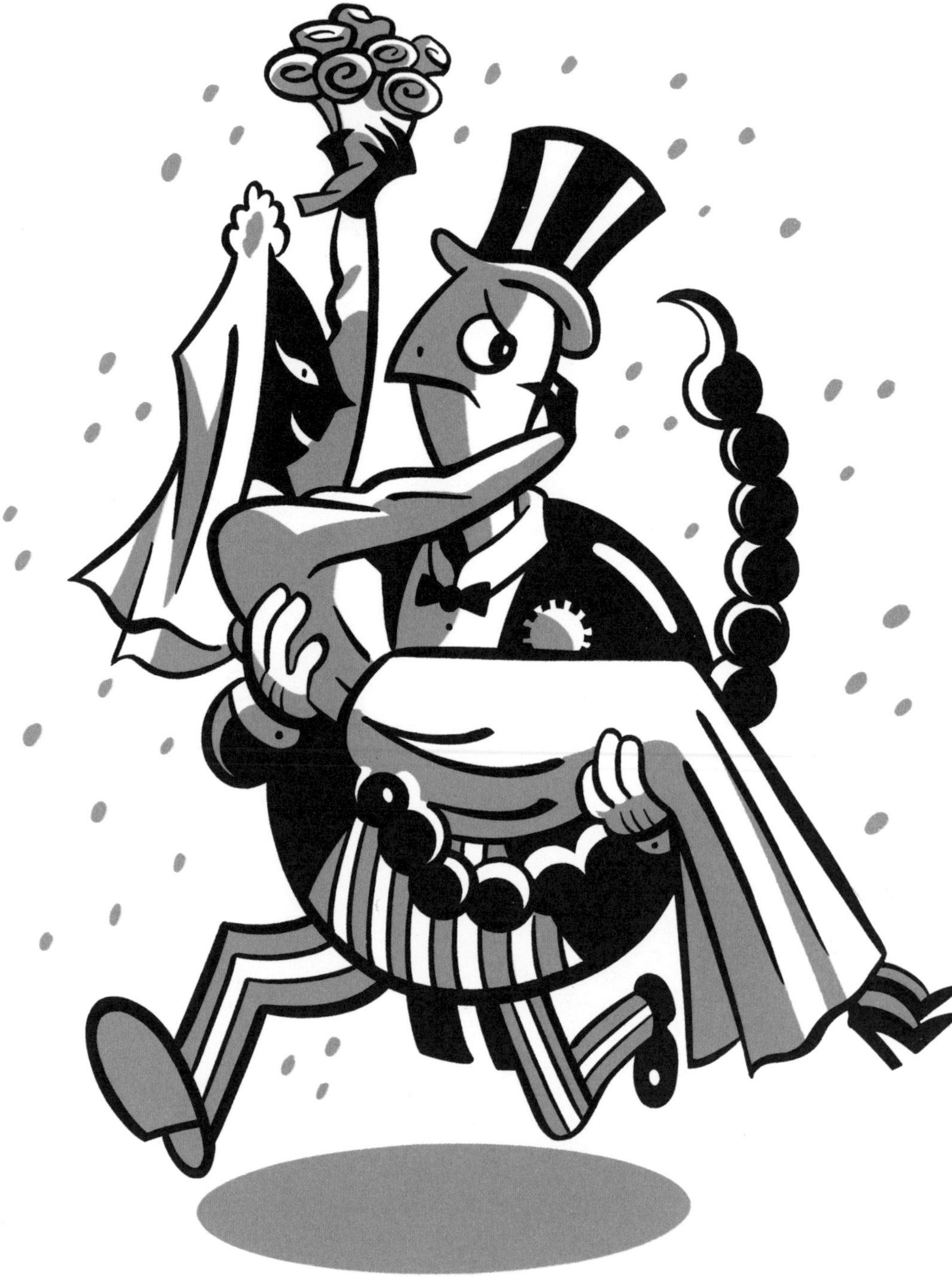

LOVE, DISHONOR, MARRY, DIE, CHERISH, PERISH

A NOVEL

David Rakoff

DOUBLEDAY

New York   London   Toronto   Sydney   Auckland

This book is a work of fiction. Names, characters, businesses, organizations, places, events, and incidents either are the product of the author's imagination or are used fictitiously. Any resemblance to actual persons, living or dead, events, or locales is entirely coincidental.

www.doubleday.com

DOUBLEDAY and the portrayal of an anchor with a dolphin are registered trademarks of Random House, Inc.

Chapters 6 and 7 of this work were previously broadcast in different form on NPR's *This American Life* in 2009 and 2003.

Book design by Chip Kidd and Michael Collica
Jacket design by Chip Kidd
Illustrations by Seth

Library of Congress Cataloging-in-Publication Data

Rakoff, David.
Love, dishonor, marry, die, cherish, perish : a novel / David Rakoff.—1st ed.
p. cm.
I. Title.
PS3618.A436L68 2013
813'.6—dc23
2012038326

ISBN 978-0-385-53521-2

MANUFACTURED IN THE UNITED STATES OF AMERICA

10 9 8 7 6 5 4 3 2 1

First Edition

For Mark Greenberg

And my family:
Vivian, Gina,
Simon, Ruth, Tom,
Micah, Amit, Asaf, and Zoe

With love everlasting.

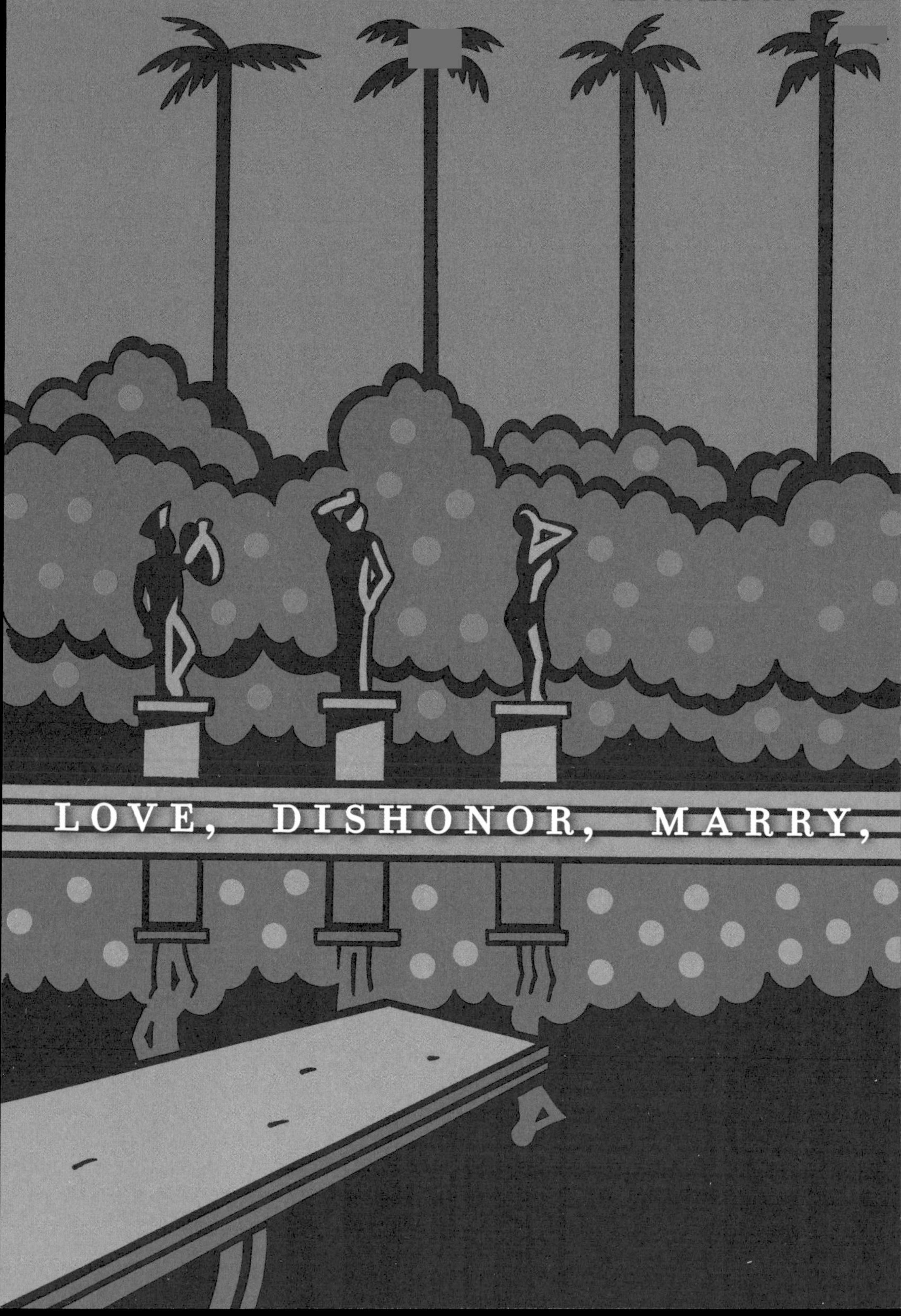
LOVE, DISHONOR, MARRY,

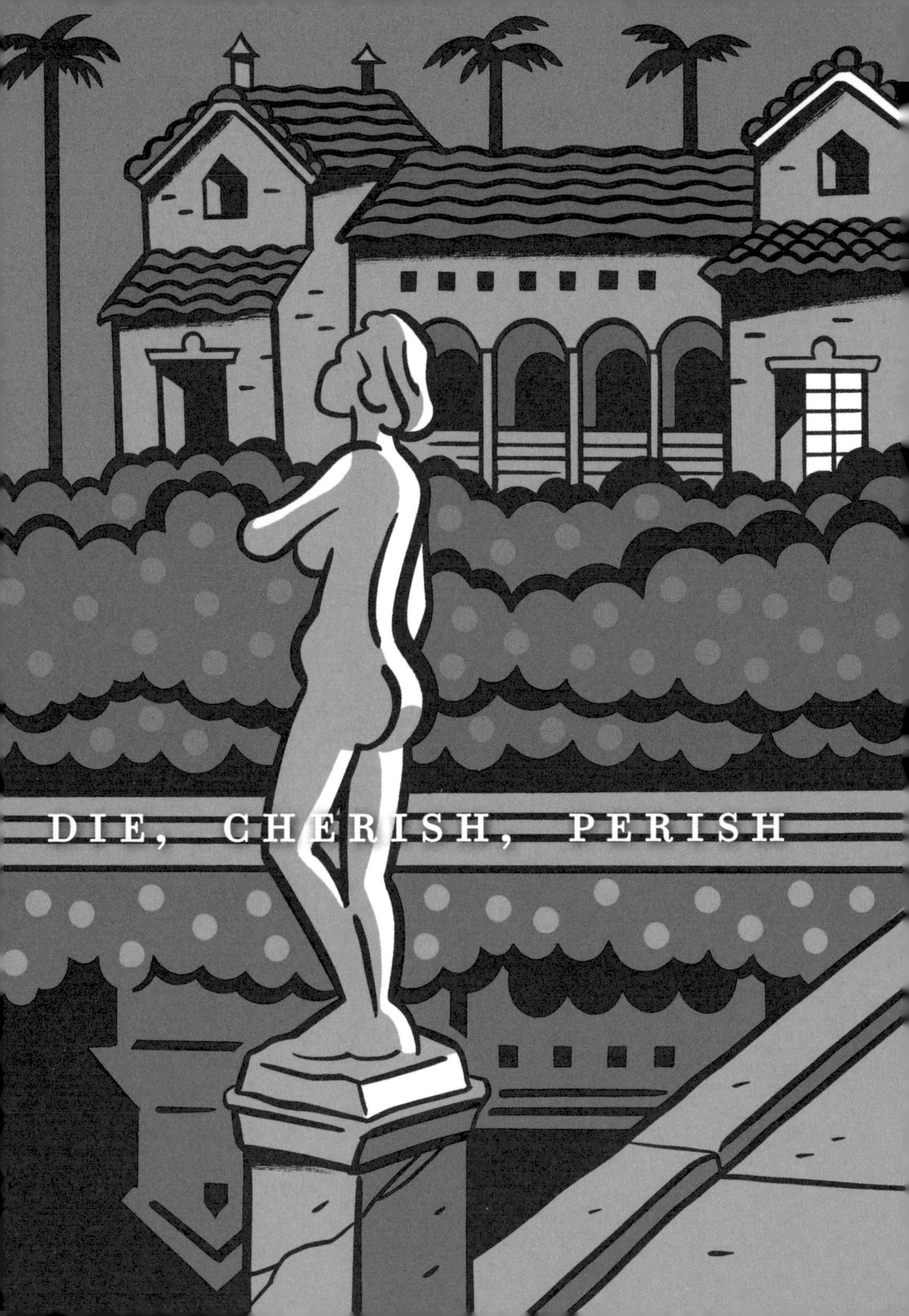

DIE, CHERISH, PERISH

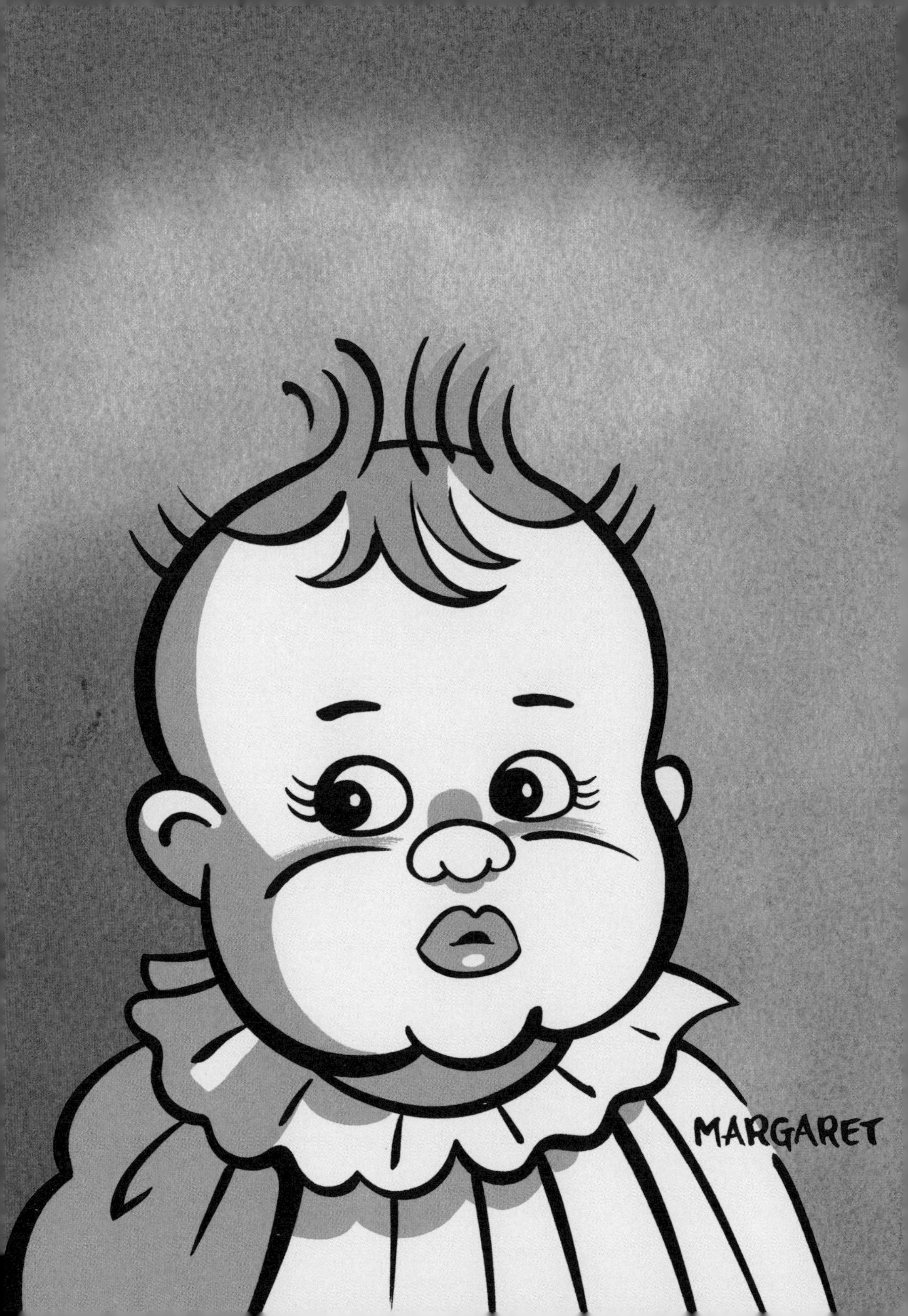
MARGARET

The infant, named Margaret, had hair on her head
Thick and wild as a fire, and three times as red.
The midwife, a brawny and capable whelper,
Gave one look and crossed herself. "God above help her,"
She whispered, but gave the new mother a smile,
"A big, healthy girl. Now you rest for a while . . ."

But later that night, with her husband in bed
The midwife gave free and full voice to her dread:
"I tell you that girl's in the grip of dark forces.
This August her husband died, trampled by horses.
She herself works on the packaging floor
But she'll be on her back for a fortnight or more.
And as for the plant, they will take her back, *maybe*
A fat lot of good is a girl with a baby,
Her story's too sad, sure, I almost can't bear it,
Nineteen-year-old widow, no family of merit.
Her mother's an *eejit*, the father a souse
Who drank away all of their money, their house.
You've seen girls like that who must go it alone,
By age twenty-five, she's a withered old crone.
Even now, she's as pale as a thing stuck with leeches,
And thin! Her dugs ought to be ripe, swelling peaches

Her milk may not come, and what comes will be gall
(She gets some food from the St. Vincent de Paul).
But true, if you ask me, I don't know what's worse:
A life full of want or a babe that's a curse.

You know me, *I* think that most infants are fair
But I've never seen so much Lucifer's Hair.
She'll grow to a strumpet, or else a virago."
Outside, thunder tore through the clouds of Chicago
And sundered the air that was needled with sleet
Although it washed clean the aroma of meat
That clung to the neighborhood's mortar and bricks,
And puddled up into the greasy, wet slicks
That, once dry, would once again smell of old blood.
To truly be clean would require Noah's flood.
Otherwise, always the smell of old carrion,
Deep as a well and as loud as a clarion.
The stockyards were too big. Each day brought a fresh
Onslaught of slaughter, and smell of dead flesh.

"You hear that?" the midwife continued. "This birth
Is bad news, proclaimed both by heaven and earth."

Margaret grew quickly, a biddable child,
Not overly sickly, her temperament mild.
As a baby, her mother would sneak her to work.
The foremen thought brats caused the women to shirk.
And so she'd stayed hidden, quite comfortably swaddled
In a nest of their overcoats. All the girls coddled

Her, stealing a kiss 'til they had to go back
To their place at the table, where daily they'd pack
Up the loins and the roasts, all the parts of the cattle
And pigs who'd been carved up, like corpses at battle.

Frankie, dubbed "Finn McCool" after the giant
Of myth, had his size, and was just as defiant;
Big as a draught-horse and strong as a steer
Frank had his enemies quaking in fear.
The tales of his strength and his temper abounded,
And God help the soul who might think them unfounded.
If Frank said that one time, in Wichita, Kansas,
He'd killed a man who had addressed him as Francis,
Or how, at the Somme, he had taken a bullet
And with his bare hands, he had managed to pull it
Straight out of his flesh . . . more's the pity for you
If you dared to venture, "But Frank, that's not true."
Even the foremen were slow to upbraid him
Though he did far less work than for what they paid him.
"Frankie will do it because Frankie can,
A law to hisself is that wall of a man!"

They'd met on the streetcar en route to the slaughter-
house, she the young widow, a six-year-old daughter,
And soon they were three, and ere long, for her sins
They'd grown now to five, with a pair of boy twins.

At school, Margaret learned basic reading and sums—
But mostly developed a hatred of nuns,

Who seemed to delight in a disciplinary
Code just as ruthless as 'twas arbitrary;
They meted out lashings and thrashings despotic
(With a thrill she would later construe as erotic):
Constance, who'd routinely knock Margaret's slate
To the floor, was monstrous and brimming with hate;
The sinister grin of old Sister Loretta
Who seemed to be driven by some old vendetta
That Margaret tried hard to appease and to fix
Although it perplexed her since she was just six.
She hoped perfect conduct might act as her savior,
But truly, no matter what Margaret's behavior,
They singled her out for particular violence,
And so she perfected a stoical silence.
"You! Red-headed terror, you want fifteen more?"
She'd shake her head slowly, her eyes on the floor.
So, when she left school at the age of eleven
To work at the factory, it seemed to her heaven.

The girls on the line who had hidden and kissed her
Welcomed her back and told her they'd missed her.
Each day she would bathe in a sea of their chatter,
Twelve-hour shifts—*standing!*—and it didn't matter;
A kerchief concealing her culpable hair,
Her mother's old shirtwaist, which thrilled her to wear.
The great roll of paper they pulled from the wall,
The huge spool of butcher's twine . . . she loved it all.
Everything seemed bathed in a heavenly light,
Perhaps, it was just as a contrast to night.

Supper, the same every day of the week:
Some contraband meat; a spleen or a cheek;
An accordion of tripe or a great, lolling tongue,
Occasional marrow bones, rare (thank God!) lung.
Both meat and the light at the close of the day
Fried wearily down to a dead, bloodless gray.
Some bread soaked in drippings. Then toilet, then prayers,
Then waiting for Frank's boots to batter the stairs.

Drink, in some men, is a beautiful thing.
Sweet Eamon Dolan finds courage to sing,
Shy William Thomas will realize he's handsome,
But Frank holds them prisoner without any ransom.
Who were you talking to? What was his name?
D'you take me for daft? Every night was the same:
Her mother would wash, while she'd dry the dishes,
Frankie would pace the room, angry, suspicious,
Occasionally some glass or plate would be broken
(Those were the lucky nights. Crockery as token).
Some mornings her mother used powder for masking
A shiner, but soon all the girls just stopped asking.

The threats go for hours. At long last he ceases
And stumbling, half-blind in his boozy paresis,
He crosses the room and falls into the bed.
Nearby, Margaret prays, "Dear God, please make Frank dead."

At twelve, Margaret grew quite suddenly bigger,
And showed the beginnings of womanly figure.

The old shirtwaists that had once fit her just right,
Had, in the wrong places, become just too tight,
Clinging and gaping where once they had hung.
Her mother was frightened, *Sure, Peg's just too young.*
The garments' constriction confirming her fears—
Though younger than Juliet's fourteen by two years—
The Romeos, pomaded, would soon come a-knocking,
Cockaded, parading. Too true, though still shocking,
Her Margaret gave off a narcotic allure,
Just how might she manage to keep her girl pure?
She tried as she could to conceal Margaret when
They had to walk past all the slaughter-floor men.

Each walk 'cross the floor was a dance of avoiding
The puddles of blood and the catcalls of "Hoyden!"
"Why all o'yer rushing? Stay back, you've got time.
My meat's not a rib, but it's certainly prime."
Each insult occasioned a new gale of laughs
They toasted each other by knocking their gaffes
Together like musketeers crossing their swords
Knee-deep in carrion but feeling like lords.
That red hair, that figure, had adult men sputtering
A wordless desire, or else they'd be muttering
Dark boasts, which a harsh glance could usually halt,
But the theme of it all was that *Peg* was at fault.
That *she* had invited, *incited* the wolfish
Responses, this siren, so stuck-up and selfish
Who had no right acting so shy and so prim
"You'd think she had diamonds all up in that quim!"

"I'll have you remember the girl is my daughter!"
Her mother would yell, but the men of the slaughter-
house would only be goaded to further chest-poundings,
Barbaric, in keeping with their vile surroundings:
The drain in the floor, a near-useless feature
Meant to dispatch all the blood of the creatures,
But gobbets of scarlet-black visceral scraps
Routinely stopped them up, clogging the traps.
Above them, hog carcasses, splayed open, red,
Like empty, ribbed, meat overcoats, overhead.

Margaret employed what she'd learned from the nuns,
Deaf to the crude innuendo and puns.
Her eyes she kept focused upon the far door,
Through which she could exit the abattoir floor.
She also employed something else the nuns taught
Her by accident: namely to fly in her thoughts
To a place close yet distant, both here and not here;
Present, but untouched by doubt or by fear.
For instance, she mused on the linguistic feat
That gave creatures names quite apart from their meat.
One didn't eat "pig," as one didn't "count muttons"
When going to sleep. Margaret thought of the buttons
From bone on her shirtwaists, her boots' good strong laces
Of rawhide, and then, Margaret pictured the faces
That daily she saw on the thousands of creatures
Their snouts notwithstanding, how human the features.
And, thinking about the brown eyes of the cattle,
She got through the door. She had skirted the battle.

Deep February, a bone-cracking freeze.
The ice, like a scythe, felled the boughs from the trees;
The blood of the stockyards froze into pink ponds
And etched the glass panes with its crystalline fronds.
"Margaret, go home," said her mother, "the group
will cover your absence. Take scraps for some soup.
Francis has fever and maybe the croup,
And Patrick this morning was all drowsy droop.
I asked Mrs. Kovacs to take the odd look . . ."
Margaret cleaned up, took her coat from the hook.
The wind was belligerent, brazen and bold.
The tram's iron tracks fairly sang in the cold.

The twins, half asleep, were reluctantly fed,
She wash-clothed their faces and put them to bed,
Before she had finished verse two of her lullaby,
They'd gone off to sleep. And now, spouting some alibi,
Frankie was there, "I come home, I was worried . . ."
He *did* seem quite nervous; more sweaty and hurried
Than his norm. "Where's yer Maw," he was able to say.
"At work, Frank. You know, as she is *every day.*"
Frankie seemed off somehow, almost confused
In his very own home. She was almost amused
Until she remembered that one would be wrong
To find any amusement in Frank for too long.

Sure enough, the change came, an invisible lever
Was pulled and a new resolve—"it's now or never"—
Put steel in his eyes and a set to his jaw,

He gripped at the jamb with a great, meaty paw.
Somehow he had managed to shake off his fright
And back was the Frank who tormented each night.
Nervousness gone, his Gibraltar-like bulk
Barring her exit, a light-blocking hulk.
"Let me pass, Frank," she whispered at almost a purr,
The way that one tries not to jangle a cur.
But Frank took ahold of her slender right wrist
And, pulling her close with a threatening twist:

"You puttin' on airs. It's always been *your* way."
He stood breathing heavily, blocking the doorway.
He twisted some more, and she screamed, "Frankie, don't."
"This is *my* house, *my* castle. Enough with 'you *won't*.'
I seen how you look at me. Thrills me to bits.
Tease me by tossing your hair, and those tits . . .
Surely this won't be the worst of your sins."
"Frankie," she wept, and implored him, "the twins!"
"You'd have me believe . . ." Frankie laughingly haggled,
His smile a dark cave of teeth, rotting and snaggled,
". . . A fast girl like you when you tell me 'it hurts!' "
While his steak of a hand bothered up Margaret's skirts.

———————

Mrs. Kovacs was sitting on Margaret's bed,
In her lap cradling the fevered girl's head.
Her mother, on seeing the petticoats, red
And torn up, thought at first that Margaret was dead.

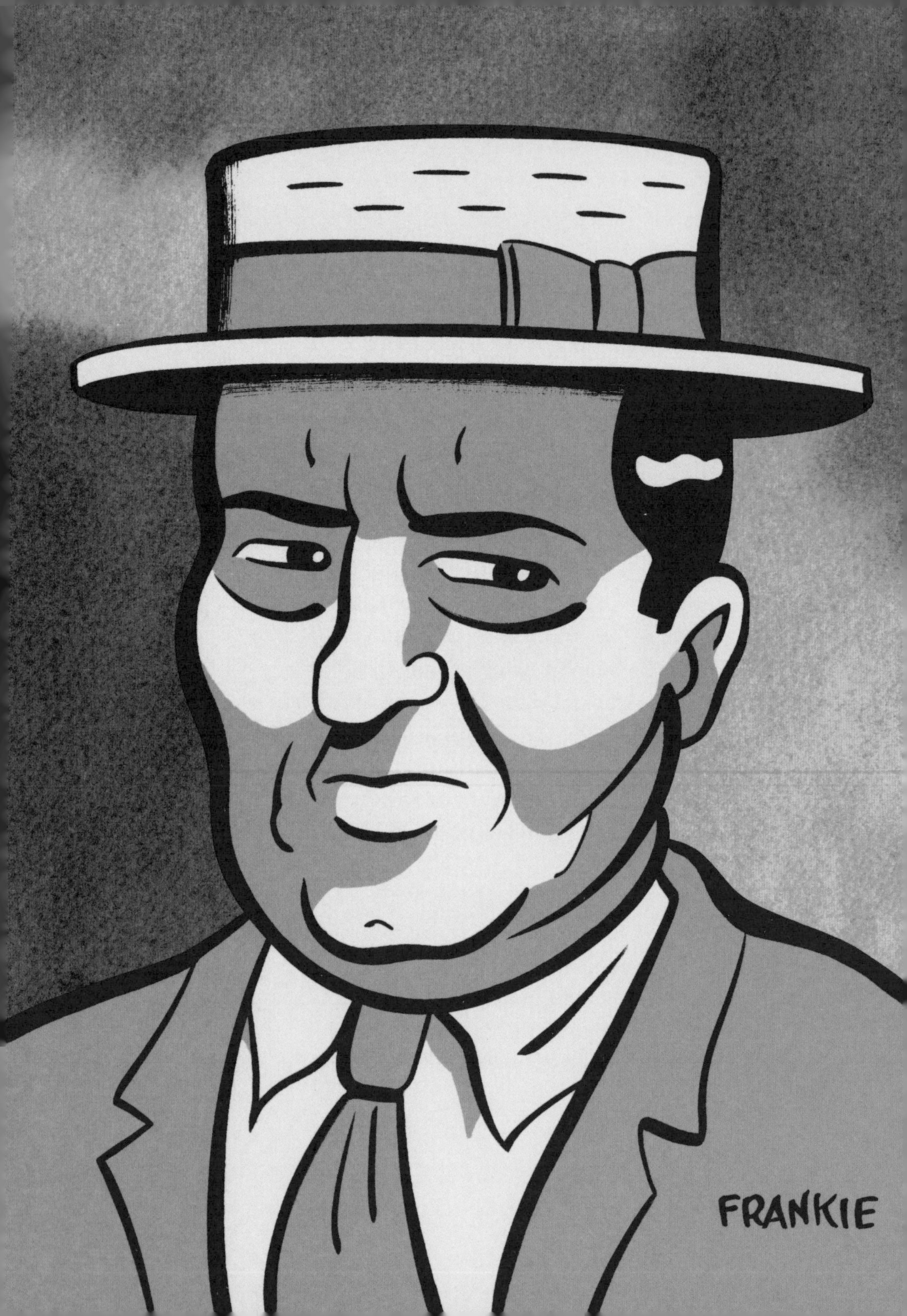
FRANKIE

"What happened?" she asked, dowsing a rag at the sink.
Kovacs, fed up, spat out, "What do you think?"
She drew herself up, "I'm sure I've no idea . . . "
She made herself haughty when things weren't clear—
She dabbed with the rag at her daughter's hot brow,
But still couldn't figure the Why or the How.
Faced with the evidence, things still never sank
In. Or wouldn't. Until Mrs. Kovacs said, "Why not ask
        Frank?"
And *still* then she chose not to see what was true,
Instead, she grabbed Peg and shrieked, "What did you do?"
"The poor girl did nothing. Your Fancy-Man Hero's
The one who was doin'. The coward. The zero."

But Kovacs should better have screamed at the wall.
Margaret's mother was lost in the thrall
Of an anger, white-hot, she had no tools to parse—
If it weren't so tragic, it could have been farce—
Her daughter no longer her charge, now her captor,
She screamed in her face, then she shook her, she slapped
        her.
"Don't dare close your eyes, Miss. We're nowhere near
        through.
I asked you, now tell me. Just. What. Did. You. *DO*?"

"Enough!" Kovacs cried. "The poor girl is senseless.
What kind of monster would beat a defenseless . . .
I come . . . as you asked me . . . to see to the boys.
I heard what I thought was a fight over toys,

But clearly, I come upon Frank unawares,
Who quickly shoved past, nearly pushed me downstairs."
"Where was Frank going?" her mother began,
But Kovacs just stopped her, "Believe me, yer man
Won't be back no time soon. And I tell you myself
If he does, I *will* call the cops. Look at her . . . Twelve!"

But to look at her daughter she now was unable.
Everywhere else—be it cupboard or table—
Seemed fine, as before, neither sullied nor tainted
But one look at Margaret, she knew she'd have fainted.
She sighed, "Filthy water will seek its own level,
What *did* I expect, with that hair o' the devil . . ."
She turned from her child, shook her head with a mutter,
"And so, as I feared, I've a girl from the gutter."

It took seven days until Frankie came back.
He'd drunk that whole week, and he'd gotten the sack.
Mrs. Kovacs never did end up calling the law
Since Margaret was five days gone, burrowed in straw
Of a western-bound boxcar, past Denver by then.
And nobody ever saw Margaret again.

Well, speaking quite strictly, not technically true.
But no one back home, no one whom she once knew.
The Margaret of Now left the Margaret Before
On a train hugging close to Lake Michigan's shore
Before peeling off on its way to the coast
Margaret, alone, with two dollars at most

Scrounged up by Mrs. Kovacs; a rye loaf with seeds,
Some sausage, a knife which, "Please God, you won't
        need."
About two hours out, in her iron-wheeled home,
And Margaret found out that she wasn't alone.
A man, dark and thin and about twenty-two-ish,
She pegged him as either a Bohunk or Jewish.
Too weak to feel fear (she was halfway to dead),
He stayed where he was, though he bowed down his head
In a gesture of most polite, courtliest greeting
As though in the dining car's first-class, first seating.
The only thing he did with any persistence
Was offer her food. Otherwise the short distance
Between them might have been the deepest of moats,
They kept to their sides, bundled up in their coats.

Until one night, rolling across the white flats
Of a snowy Dakota, the barely-there slats
Of the car were no match for the blizzard outside.
Margaret was simply unable to hide
From the cold so severe she feared she might die
And there was the man now beside her. "Let I . . ."
He said, stuffing straw into all of the cracks,
He lay down, pulling Margaret in, molding her back
To his front, then enfolding her, so that she'd feel
His warmth while he whispered, repeated, "*Sha, Schtil* . . ."
And soon Margaret slept in the train's gentle quaking,
But warm and relaxed and no longer shaking.
His song was a comfort, a womb she could bundle in.

But no meaning at all: "*Rozhinkes . . . Mandlen . . .*"
She woke the next morning, the train briefly parked
To take on supplies. Her friend had disembarked.
From then on until Margaret reached her destination
The cold didn't manage the same penetration.

If in '28, you had chanced by the water
Of Seattle's harbor, you might spy three daughters
Working alongside two sons and a mother
And dad, you would see something lovely and other:
The father, a raven-haired man, Japanese,
The mother, with hair like the autumnal trees,
And children just Western enough so's to pass
With tresses the color of bright polished brass.
The wife wraps your fish, gives you one of her smiles,
But her eyes tell a journey of thousands of miles.
And in the Midwest, a babe pulled from the loins
Has a head full of curls shining like copper coins,
And the midwife is twigged to a child from years back
But there've been *so* many babies, by now she's lost track.

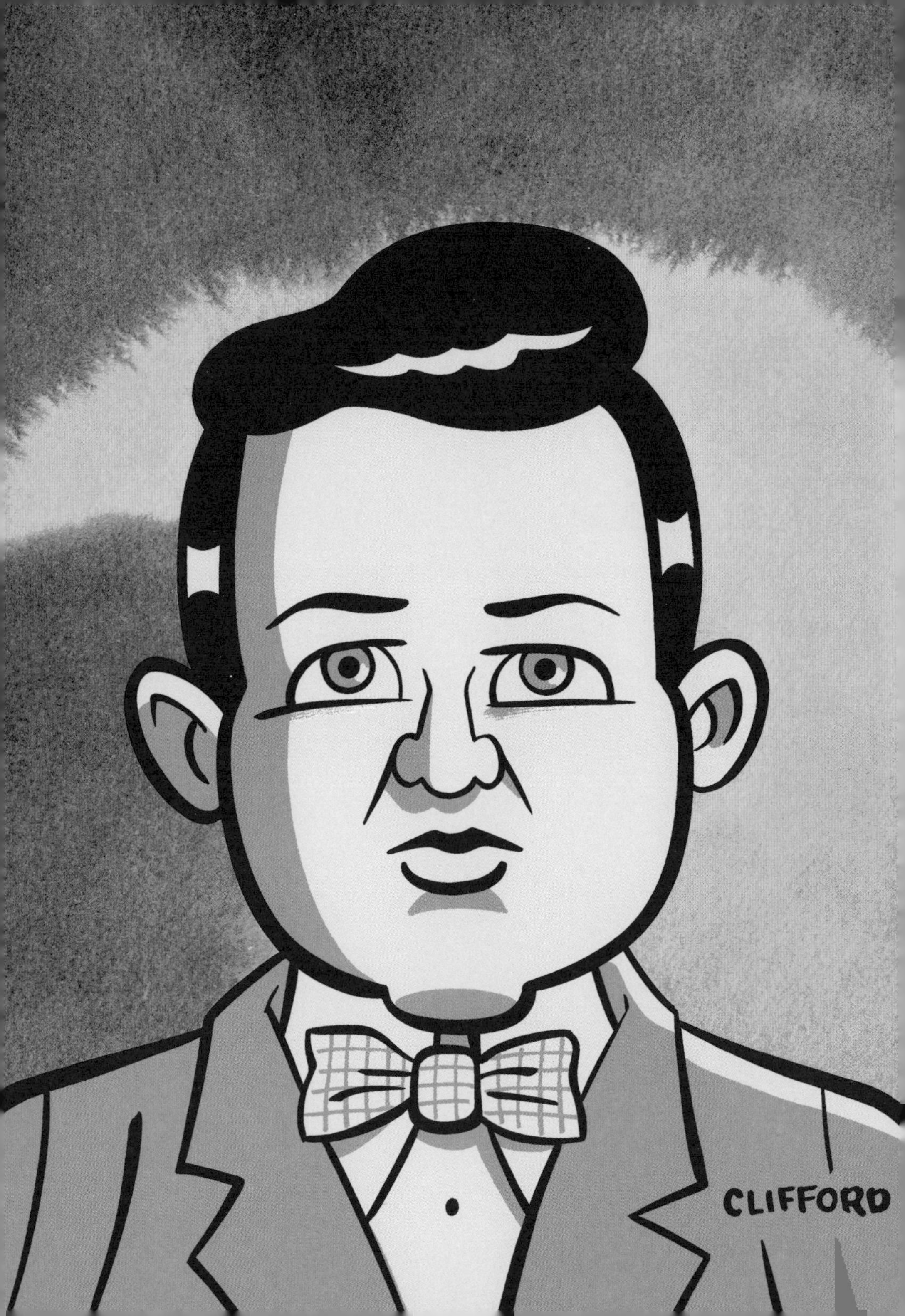
CLIFFORD

"To pay for what crime, what malfeasance, what sin?"
Clifford's mother mused, picking her blouse from her skin.
"Malibu's breezy, Hollywood's shady
But Burbank? He might as well've brought us to Hades!
I could just yip when I think of the crime it
Was moving me out here *because of the climate.*"
The fan in her hand the scene's sole, languid motion,
"I once heard it said that there was an ocean
Not terribly distant from where we sit here,
But, I suppose that was just a bum steer.
Escaping me now are the details specific,
But could it be named something like 'The Pacific'?"
Her voice was dramatic, befitting her role
Of a truth-telling wag: witty, gin-dry, and droll.

She reasoned it thus: that it surely beat weeping
And couldn't help smiling with how out of keeping
It was with the truth of her fate-handed cards
Her down-at-heel block with its sun-roasted yards
She found it amusing and helped pass the day
To speak like a guest at a fancy soiree,
She battled the hours without end with a heightened
Insouciance, like whistling when, truly, one's frightened.
With steely resolve she kept up this appearance

Her husband no more than a mild interference
The way one might greet less than optimal weather.
His half-palsied body? As light as a feather!
Diminishing powers of speech, what a scream!
Feeding and grooming (hours each), *such* a dream.
It might take all morning to just get him showered
And yet one might think she had married Noël Coward
Such *teddibly* juicy, just-so bits of news
With witty, urbane, *comme il faut* aperçus.
Even though it was usually just she and her son
Who, though six, proved a rapt audience of one.

She sat on the porch with her thousand-yard stare
And spent each day parked in her old wicker chair.
The yard a brown painting of motionless calm
The packed, ochre dirt and the lone, scraggly palm.
No sway to its fronds nor the measly dry grasses,
Immobile and baking in air like molasses.
Nearby was the car, having one was a must,
A '38 Packard, near silver with dust.
Her husband had needed it when he was traveling
But that, too, was part of the wholesale unraveling
Of what had once been a not-horrible life,
But now here she was, neither widow nor wife
Like flies trapped in amber, the three of them stuck
Like so many others dealt cards of rough luck.

Clifford, attempting to shake off her blues,
Might draw her a hat or a new pair of shoes:

A bonnet fantastic, bombastic, and huge, he
Appended three veils and a tiny Mount Fuji.
Pumps clasped with diamonds and marabou trimming
And thick soles of glass, housing live goldfish, swimming!
His mother surveyed his designs with a laugh,
"If I wore these both, I would be a giraffe."

He lived for her laughter and after that how
She might rustle the fine hair that fell 'cross his brow.
"You have scads more talent, beyond any other
Kid I've ever seen, and I'm not just your mother.
I'm a good judge of art." With her fingers she gaveled
The armrest. "I've seen things. Remember, I've traveled."

Remember she'd traveled? As if he'd forget.
Her life before him was the thing that beget
His voracious desire and unquenchable fond-
ness for all the world's beauty that lay just beyond
Their veranda enclosed in its old fly-flecked screen.
Cliff sometimes felt like the one who had been.

The Great War concluded a scant two years prior.
They'd sailed to a Europe no longer on fire,
"Our trunks bore initials with golden embossing
A French tutor booked for each day of the crossing
And Father tipped porters with whole silver dollars!
I had a wool coat with a beaver-fur collar,
And *dresses*! A new one for each day at sea
Not counting the outfits we'd change after tea

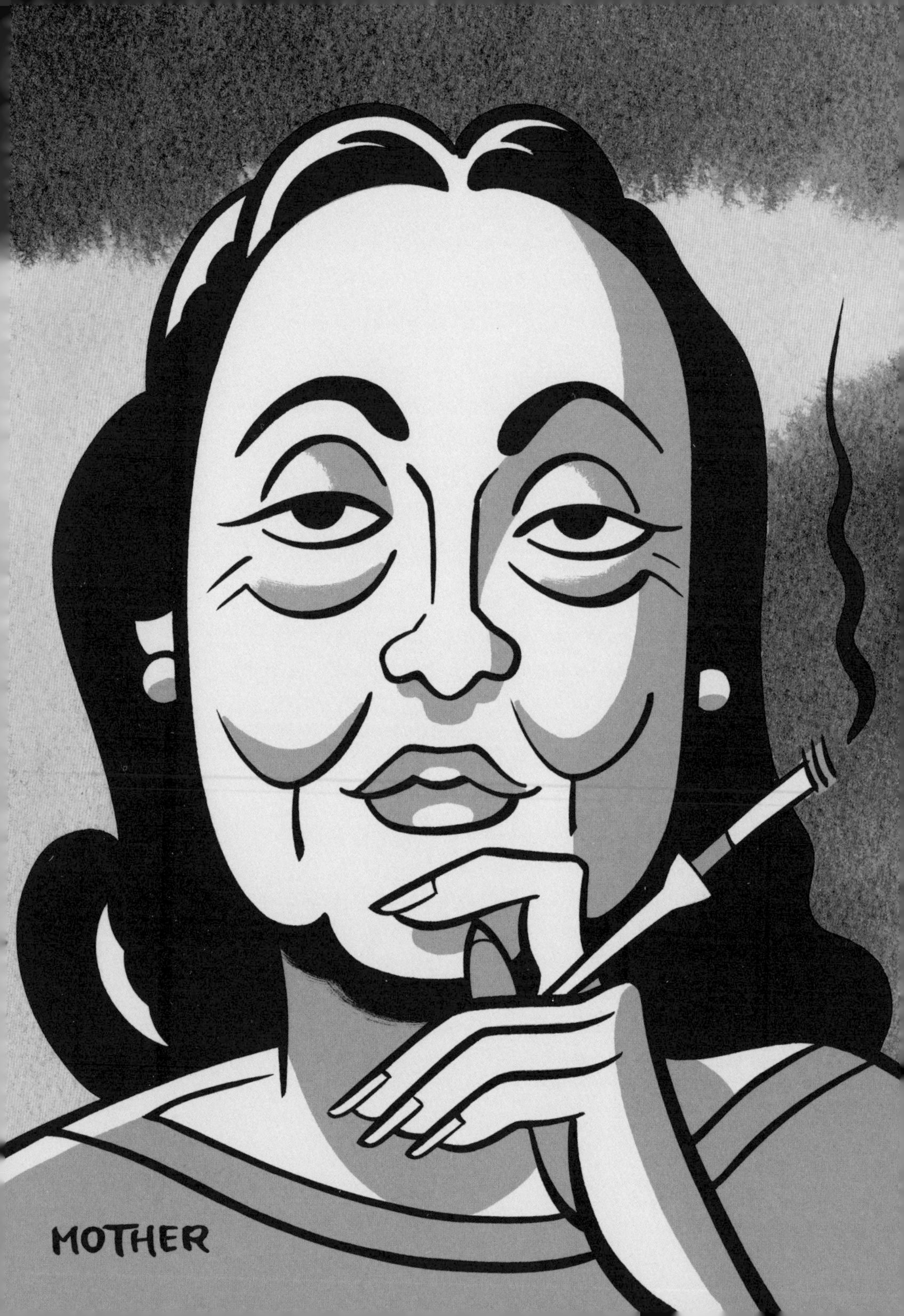
MOTHER

And for each ensemble, a different purse!"
(Clifford had memorized chapter and verse.)

"He was so profligate, heedless, and rash.
It's quite a feat how, with no help from the Crash
How easily parted our gold from that fool
By '26 Sally and I had to leave school."
As with all else, she would choose to be funny
About how her father had squandered his money:
"And all of us crammed in that one narrow row house.
If not for our wages, there would have been no house.
Last I heard, Father was down on the Bowery,
A whole mess of bother and woe was my dowry.
Your grandfather, Clifford, could sure make a mess
Of a perfectly good situa . . . I digress.

Fish knives and cake forks, and gleaming tureens!
Truly, your aunt and I ate like young queens.
New Year's on board was all revel and roister-
ing. Crackers with prizes, and champagne with oysters."
Each knot from the shore, she could feel adolescence
Depart in the wake's churning, green phosphorescence,
And churning in *her* was, as if by duress,
An appetite—bone deep—a need to transgress.
The evenings were worse, once the supper bell rang,
The darkness, the wine, well, her blood fairly sang.
"A dark Turkish ensign gave me my first kiss,"
And then she paused, "Should I be telling you this?
Ah, might as well learn," she went on with a shrug,

"His tongue in my mouth was a slimy, fat slug.
I remember I thought to myself, 'Holy Jesus,
This will *not* be worth it unless Father sees us.' "

With deepest conviction she found near hilarious
Clifford stopped viewing the trip as vicarious.
Studying programs, the postcards, the scraps,
He fingered the flyers and mangled the maps
An El Greco folio she'd kept from the Prado
A stub from the D'Oyly Carte's thrilling *Mikado*
She'd tied to a Soho-bought gilt ivory fan,
(He counted the two as a stop in Japan).
Above all, the thing that had captured his heart,
And opened his world: reproductions of art.
Bernini and Rubens, Poussin and David
They filled Clifford with a near-physical need
To render as best as he could all he saw
The only desire Clifford had was to draw,
To master the methods the artist commands
That translate a thing from the eye to the hands.
There might be a hint in the dry introductions
He'd flip back between them and the reproductions.
Clifford consumed them as if they were food;
He studied how color might render a mood
Skin tone and placement, drapery and flowers
Moonlight on lovers asleep beneath bowers
Torments endured with a saint's skyward smile
Nuance, technique, composition, and style.

Landscapes with dream-like blue hills in the distance,
The Sabine's dramatic, up-reaching resistance
Of strong Roman arms that were trying to rape her,
His greasy young fingers had yellowed the paper.
The jam smears and markings and smudges and rips
All left in the scrapbooks she'd kept of her trips.
Souvenirs treasured like they were his own,
He swore that he'd go there as well once he'd grown.
"Make sure to say yes, then, if anyone offers,
Since there's not a *sou* in the family coffers."

She gave up entirely the impulse to say,
"It's lovely out, Cliffie, why don't you go play?"
And play where, exactly? The yard was an eyesore,
(They'd seen in a newsreel, a famine in Mysore,
Identical dirt turned to similar mud,
A sacred cow chewing its sad, holy cud
Flies crawling over a child's thin, dry face,
She heard Clifford whisper, "That's just like my place!").
He liked it indoors where, dark as a séance,
Hunched over his sketchbook with pencil and crayons
And sprawled on the carpet in front of the wireless
He filled up the pages, his output was tireless.

Amethyst asters on brown banks of peat,
Aloes with leaves thick and fleshy as meat.
Beryl-eyed lions and gray monkeys who so
Resembled the creatures of *Le Douanier Rousseau*.

Succulents' paddles and dew-heavy fronds,
Tourmaline fish swam through indigo ponds,
Ivies that twined with a grip near prehensile . . .
All sprang alive from the tip of Cliff's pencil.
Inspired by his *Child's Book of Fauna and Flora*
And broadcasts of *Rex Bond, Inveterate Explorer!*

O Rex! Weekly captured or worse, left for dead
In faraway places that filled Clifford's head
Rex could escape from the direst of rotten spots
Bloodthirsty tigers or cannibal Hottentots,
Meeting his end in the desert, the drink,
Tsetse flies, quicksand, or thrown in the clink
Left on a newly calved iceberg, adrift
But lately the perils had made a slight shift.
Fictional savages, strange voodoo mystics
Supplanted by dangers far more realistic.
Now Japs with their cunning, or Jerries with Mausers
Tried, but could not muss the crease of his trousers.
"For boys, just remember, the fieriest blitz
Is no match against our American wits!
Stay alert and stay wise to all foreign-born knavery.
Show grit and resolve and mimic the bravery
Of all of our men on the land, air, and sea
Who continue to fight so that we may be free!
When a threat rears its head, don't shrink and don't cower
Just rise to the challenge, like Amber Wave Flour!
Takes recipes meager and renders them rich,
If eager for tender cakes, Mother should switch!

And remember, the dawn comes when things seem most
    bleak,
Good night, boy and girls, and please tune in next week!"

There's little as scalding as juvenile ardor.
It's quickening as hatred or anger, but harder
To parse, 'specially when one must feign not to covet
One's heart's one desire, one's secret beloved
Since others might feel it was somehow unsuitable
So you become guarded, sphinx-like, inscrutable.
But sleep—free of judgment—knits care's raveled sleeve.
In slumber, without so much as "by your leave,"
Was Clifford allowed certain muscles to flex
And truly be all that he could to dear Rex.
A Rex, needing rescue, who'd sent an alert
To Clifford, uniquely equipped to avert
A numinous, formless, Rex-threat'ning disaster
Conspiring to injure his muscular master.
He'd find Rex bound up in some old, empty warehouse
And carry him home (in the dream it was *their* house)
He'd bathe him and generally salve the abuses
By pressing his lips to incipient bruises.
Until, the repletion near up to the hilt, he
Would waken quite shaken and sweaty (and guilty),
To find that his mother was calling his name . . .
So back to the world of his clandestine shame.

——————

"I may well be shrewd, but not 'shrewish,' " she'd titter,
By which she meant not irretrievably bitter;
Twelve years and counting, still able to joke
Despite her sick husband, quite corkscrewed with stroke.
And truly she was shrewd, had practical knowledge
And worked in the local community college
Keeping the books, a quite valuable service
The dean told her numbers had made him quite nervous.
And thanks to her privileged employee's status
She put Cliff in Life Drawing, totally gratis.
"It's each Monday night for three hours," she told
Him, "it's serious, no joking, your classmates are old.
And though you're fifteen, you will *still* be the best.
Just wait, they'll be bug-eyed, bedazzled, impressed.
And soon you'll draw bodies just like as you see 'em,
It's this class today and tomorrow, museum!
But Cliffie," she said—yes she really was shrewd—
"The models you draw you will draw in the nude."
And paying close heed to her dear son's reflexes,
She added "Nude men *and* women, it is both sexes."
And there it was! An almost invisible thing
Like seeing a breeze or a hummingbird's wing,
The mention of men had gone straight to his heart
And her son gave an almost electrical start
Which caused within *her* some invisible flower
To bloom, because dear ones, all knowledge is power.

Of course she was right, Cliff drew circles around
All the others, and what's more, he happily found

His *talent* his most pronounced characteristic,
Not "longhair" or "pansy" or other sadistic
Abuse, instead he was now deemed "The Professor."
And his youth made him safe, he was also confessor:
Marie, whose red thermos contains scotch and water,
Barbara who hates that she hates her own daughter,
Dan's sorrow masked by the face of a bon vivant,
Clifford stayed silent like any good confidant.
Grown-ups, it seemed, were quite blithely un-curious,
A silence and safety Cliff found quite luxurious
Their secrets would never expand to a chat.
He would listen, was young, he could draw, that was that.

And as for the drawing, he loved the deep rigor
Demanded of him, he attacked with new vigor
The honing of skill, lines were finer, less crude
It registered barely that subjects were nude.
The occasional breast, due to space, time, and gravity
Might give a brief shock, but there was no depravity
Nor any great interest about what was there
He was frankly relieved for the chevron of hair
Concealing some deeper and unwanted knowledge,
Until one day Paul, on the track team at college,
Posed and put Cliff through the sufferings of Job
The instant he untied and took off his robe.

His limbs like the *David*'s, impossibly fine,
And lacing just under like flesh-covered twine
The veins that gave life to this ambulant art,

Shunting blood from his (sure to be beautiful) heart
'Cross the shoulders and down to the backside's deep cleft,
To his manhood that hung with imperious heft,
To the ribs, blue with shade 'neath his chest's cantilever,
Cliff was undone as if he'd caught a fever.
His charcoal went wide in an anarchic scrawl
Clifford felt hot, cold, then started to fall
He heard someone laugh, as though this was a game
Then he blacked out as everyone shouted his name.

Infirmary couch, with its cool, ox-blood Naugahyde
Clifford felt boneless and battered and raw inside.
A verdict passed down that could not be revoked,
Something was loosed that felt formerly choked;
A process, unstoppable, once it began
Like trying to put shaving cream back in its can.
A vaguely elating but frightening bubble,
He felt buoyant and free and yet somehow in trouble.
In excess of caution, they'd summoned his mother
And asked her, concerned, had there been any other
Such fevers of late, whether he had been sick,
"His head hit the floor like a cloth-covered brick."
They told her that it had been Paul who had carried him
(Cliff, dimly conscious, thought they'd said *married* him).
Surveying this savior, she said with a stealthy
Murmur that no one could hear, "*He* seems healthy."
Clifford seemed fine, all were happy, relieved.
He was no worse for wear, and the others believed

That the culprit was likely the heat of the room
To which Clifford's mother responded with "Hmmm . . ."

Children's illogic can be an exquisitely
structured mistake. Take Aunt Sally's visit:
Each May Clifford's mother took two weeks off work
For her sister and niece who would come from New York.
They'd go meet their train (Cliff inspecting their berth)
Then back to the house for a fortnight of mirth.
Albums to leaf through, plus meals to eat. After
They'd sit on the porch, both exploding with laughter
From nonsense, like asking "How big were his feet?"
About a man Sally had seen on the street.
Everything lilted or swooped with their joking,
Baby talk always accompanied smoking:
"Weach fow a Wucky inthtead of a thweet!"
Eyes bugged and lips smacked. Oh, what a rare treat!
His mother's delivery, so usually brusque
Would, during those visits—especially near dusk—
Ooze sultry and slower and wooze on the brink
Of the " 'D'-to-'J' journey" (where "drink" becomes
        "jrink").
The change wasn't only confined to their speech:
Everything that came within Sally's reach
Seemed somehow transformed, and largely because
Of just her, like when the house landed in Oz.

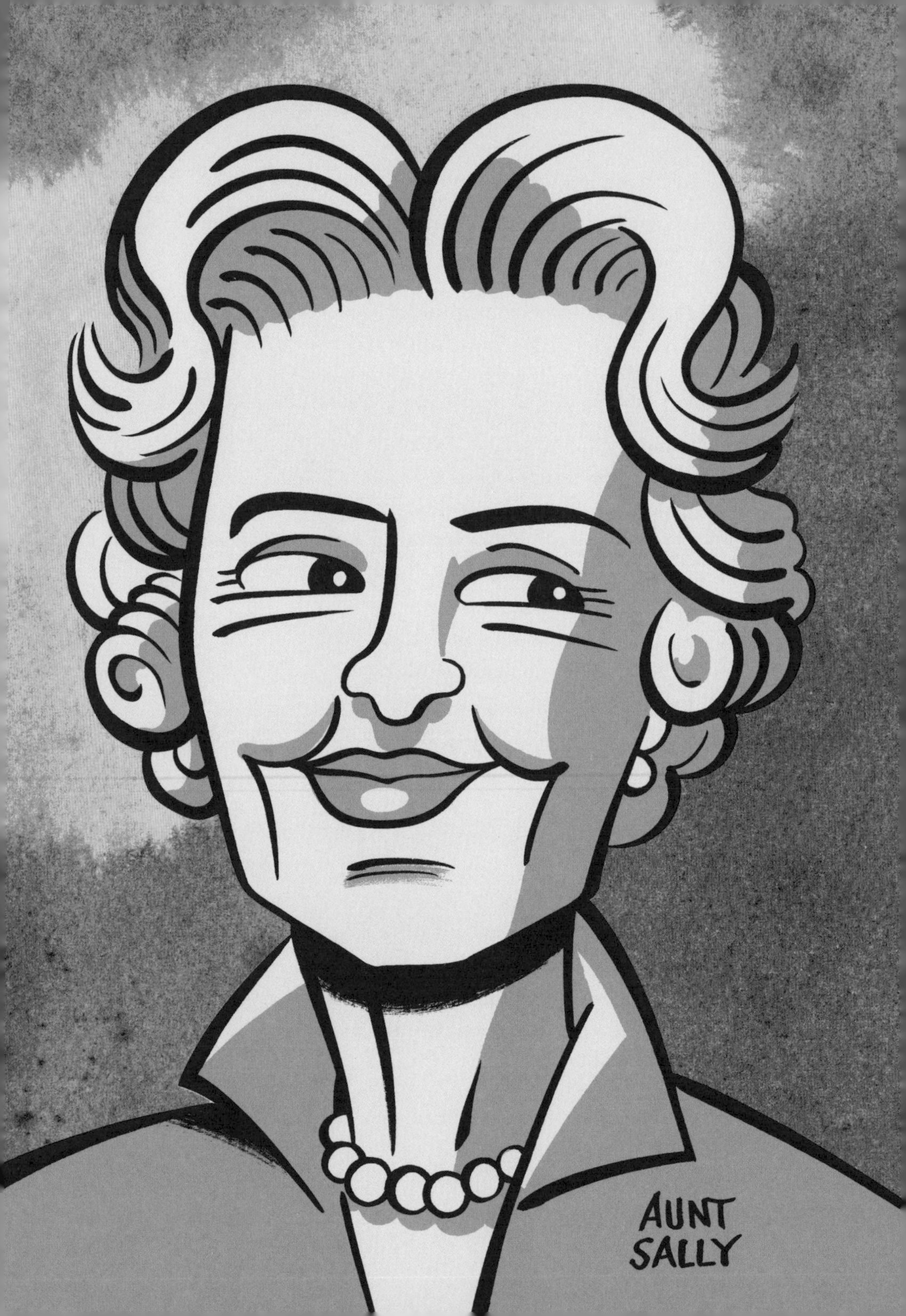
AUNT SALLY

Prior and post, life could hardly be duller
But during! The world buzzed in bright Technicolor.
An adverb of joy, to his six-year-old thinking,
To "do it 'Auntsally' " meant action plus drinking,
Ice cream for breakfast and socks never matching!
Bark like a dog for a fierce tummy-scratching.
There was none of the darkness that can come with alcohol.
Just a delightful ignoring of protocol.

As he grew older, he realized the frivolous
Nature hid goodness that bordered on chivalrous.
Sally was truly the bestest of eggs,
She'd spend hours massaging the chicken-bone legs
Of Cliff's unresponsive but darting-eyed father,
She'd keep up the chatter, like it was no bother
"There you are, Hiram. As handsome as ever."
Her kindness encased in a varnish of clever,
She'd talcum his feet, or bring in fresh flowers,
Read him a *Photoplay* for what seemed like hours.

———————

"For what seemed like hours," while always subjective
Was now so unknowable, flimsy, selective,
In thrall to the twists of his brain's involutions
The cranial mists and synaptic occlusions
He'd had to contend with since he'd had his stroke,
Like trying to sculpt something solid from smoke.

Everything now: liquid Space, rubber Time,
Tenuous grasps of both reason or rhyme
Could now trap his words in a Mobius loop,
He'd spent a whole day thinking "Elegant Soup"
(Despite that no broth was remotely forthcoming
And how could it be that his knees would be humming?
Or buzzing? Bees' Knees? {Be Sneeze!}). So confusing
Hours might go by in such meaningless musing.

Hiram was Hirschl, of that he was certain—
Though other details were obscured by a curtain
Of knowledge he no longer knew if he knew,
So, Hiram was Hirschl, and Hirschl is . . . you?
Hirschl came more than three decades before,
A lead to some landsman outside Baltimore
Had failed to achieve a reliable connection,
And so in the *Forverts's* classified section,
From Bozeman, Montana, a dry goods concern:
"Be ready to work and be willing to learn."

And so with no warning and no indication,
The years concertina'd; expansion, deflation . . .
Images atomized, sudden dispersals
Time barreled forward, loped back through reversals,
And now, from some darkest recess of his brain
A vision—long-lost—of The Girl on the Train.

He'd come upon others while riding the rails
But no one that young, nor as haunted or frail.

And hair! Surely reddest hair he ever saw
He'd briefly thought there was a fire in the straw.
Out there alone, barely thirteen years old
Such shaking! And not only due to the cold.

She knew, in some way, that he meant her no harm
And silently slid herself into his arms.
To try to allay any feelings of skittish-
ness, he rocked her to sleep with an old song in Yiddish.
"Raisins and almonds," "A little white goat,"
She burrowed herself in the depths of his coat.

Clifford is here now, his good, gentle child,
He'd love nothing more than to be able to smile,
To look at the drawings Cliff spread 'cross the bed,
Be anything but unresponsive, half dead
Perhaps the return of this strange, red-haired flower
Is simple nostalgia for when he had power.

"Let's let him sleep, Cliff." Sally turns out the light.
Hirschl stares forward at nothing all night.

———————

The only plant Sally's bright light failed to nourish
Was Helen, her daughter, too timid to flourish.
And Sally's attempts were, quite frankly, misguided,
Always a cut-up, she joshed and she chided
And went on and on at uncomfortable length

Thinking (in error) that Helen had strength
To be able to laugh, or at least grasp the gist
That the jests were at scars whose wounds did not exist.
In this regard, Helen was tone-deaf. Fantastic
Untruths sounded real, not the least bit sarcastic.
Ah, but tone deafness shuttles in any direction;
To Sally, the japing was naught but affection.
She had no idea that her joking fell flat,
That calling her slender girl "Porky" and "fat"
Or just outright fictions like, "*Try* not to limp,"
Made Helen curl inward: a cowed, sheepish shrimp.
Constantly braced for harsh words or cold looks,
Perpetually hunched, as if carrying books
With titles like *Helen, the Girl No One Wanted.*
Cliff felt the bond of the outcast, the taunted.

Where he had been strengthened almost to unbreakable
(By sketching his tormentors' torments unspeakable)
She was contrite, too polite, over-dutiful
Never aware that, in truth, she was beautiful.
Taller, it's true, than a girl ought to be,
Boys, when they looked, called her "Flagpole" or "Tree,"
But Clifford could see with an eye almost clinical—
Yet open, affectionate, not at all cynical—
The classic proportions informing her shape.
It was all he could do not to grab her and drape
Her in bedsheets as toga, and once he had made
That, he'd ringlet her hair with a daub of pomade.

And Helen would let him, though she, two years older,
Felt Clifford was wiser than she, he was bolder,
With deeply held views on all manner of things:
Mustard (No!), Claude Monet (Yes!), cabbages, kings.
When they were young, they'd begun each trip shyly—
Regarding the other suspiciously, slyly—
Until, not unlike the way both of their mothers
Resumed their old bond, quite impervious to others,
By Day Two, to see them, it would have seemed quibbling
To call them just cousins. They acted like siblings.
And though his allegiance was chief to his art
She felt he had only her interests at heart.
She never felt his deep absorption neglect, nor
Ever stopped feeling he was her protector.
If Clifford proposed it, she'd echo with "Me, too!"
To things she'd have otherwise never agreed to.

To wit: behind privets and glinting like jewels
Lay largely unguarded cerulean pools.
All maintained perfectly, pristine as new,
Temptingly empty, impossibly blue.
The owners, at country homes up in the mountains,
Cared little, it seemed, for the frothing of fountains
Nor for the colonnades, marble, mosaic
(A rectangle would have been far too prosaic),
The plaster Poseidons on acanthus plinths,
Friezes aswirl with young mermaids and nymphs
All lay unnoticed, unloved, un-enjoyed,
How could they not but dive into this void?

Daily—when either was seized by the whim—
They'd slip through the hedges and go for a swim.
Make free with the towels in poolside cabanas,
And eat from the trees: mangoes, loquats, bananas.
One time they'd both scrambled up into trees
And stayed well concealed 'til the old Japanese
Man who tended the grounds had passed by out of sight.
Helen had never felt such thrilling fright.
She'd all but stopped breathing, so's not to arouse
The gardener's gaze up into the green boughs.
The coast clear, she clambered to earth and then joined
Clifford, his arms full of fruit he'd purloined.

"Take these," he said, filling her arms with the loot
That he'd pulled from the branches. Now laden with fruit,
Clutching them all to her rubberized bodice
Clifford regarded her, whispering "Goddess."
The bright orange globes did their best to defeat her,
And fall from the grasp of their poolside Demeter.
"Cliffie, they're dropping, there must be a dozen . . ."
She started to say, but was stopped by her cousin
With a quietly stern admonition, "Don't talk, I
Just need to compose you." His black Brownie Hawkeye
The charm, like a mesmerist's watch on a chain
Helen fell silent and wondered again
How Clifford could somehow just know how to take light
And coax magic into a box of black Bakelite.
Moving her under an arch of white flowers
Artist and muse worked together for hours.

Dismissing some poses as "striving for cute,"
Clifford said softly, "Now roll down your suit."
He gave her a couple of oranges, "Here."
And showed her just how she should hold up each sphere.
His voice held no sneer nor a trace of a jest.
She trusted him fully that baring her chest
Would make the best pictures. She laughed when she saw
The inside-out breasts of the cups of the bra.
"Keep laughing," he said, didn't need to ask twice;
She felt so secure and the breeze felt so nice.
They worked thirty minutes or so, 'til the sun
Started to set, at which Clifford said, "Done."
Back through the hedge to the house where they let
Sally juice the "breasts" for crêpes suzette.

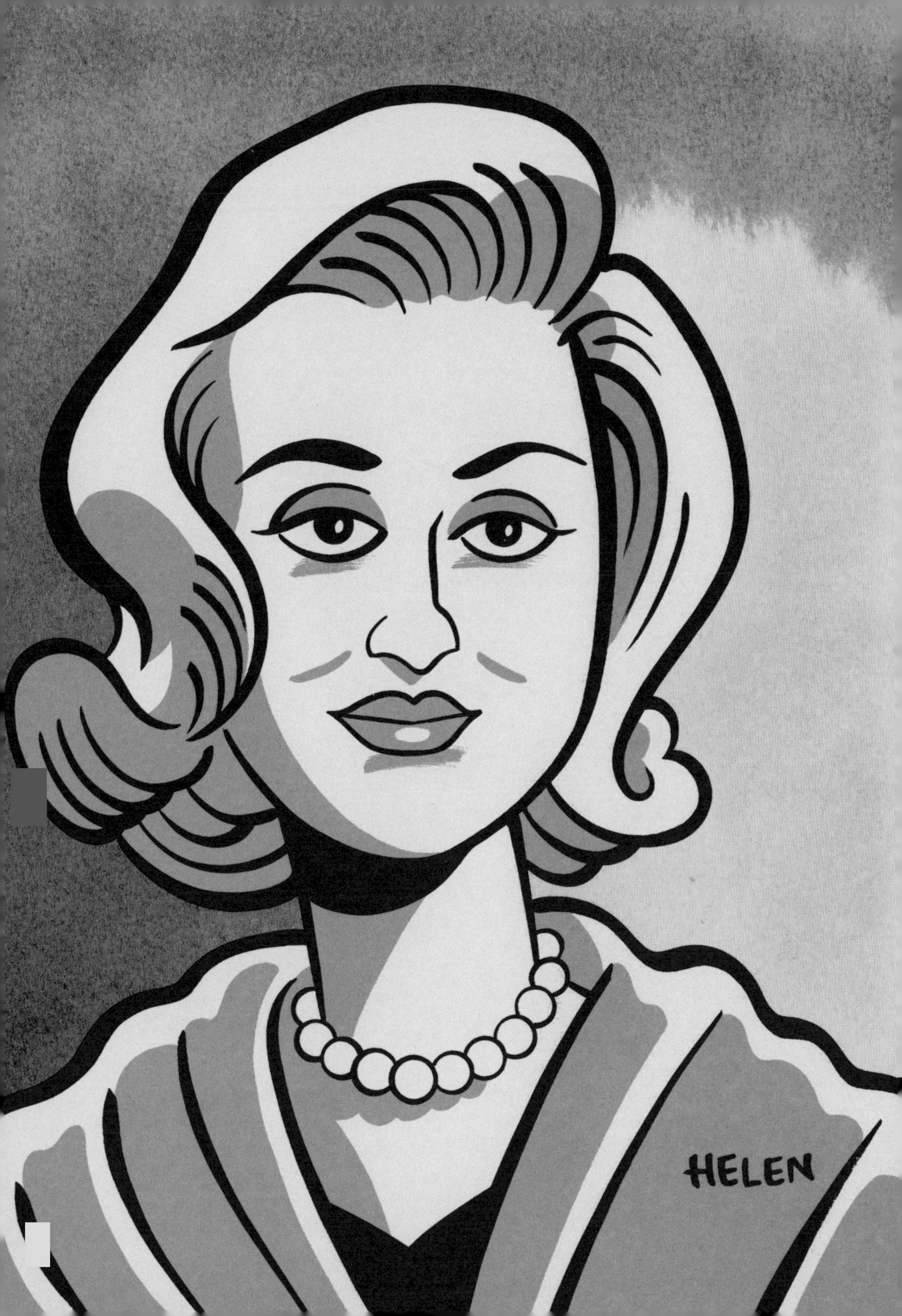
HELEN

Ten a.m. in December in midtown Manhattan,
Helen sits at her desk in a dress of blue satin.
A pearl among swine, so at odds with the bustling
Of mid-morning business, her taffeta's rustling.
A vision of cocktails in coffee-break light.
She is garbed for the company party that night.
It is too far a trek out to Avenue J,
Just to go home to change at the end of the day,
So she sits, doing work, ignoring the mounting
Whispers and jokes, led by Kay in Accounting.
She's aware that her dress makes the other girls laugh
As they congregate over the mimeograph.
Helen gamely endures not the kindest of stares,
With aplomb, for you see, Helen no longer cares.
Well, that's mostly the truth. Though some doubts still
      impinge
Each year 'round Thanksgiving, an unwelcome twinge
Starts to niggle and rankle and by mid-December
She wonders anew, *Do they all still remember?*
Helen turns a blind eye to the smirks and the winks.
Surely it's not still about <u>that</u>, she thinks.

Time's gone by since that silly, regrettable business
When she became known as The Girl Who Ruined Christmas.

Helen harbors the hope that the passing five years
Have made folks forget both the vomit and tears
And throwing of glassware and drunken oration,
That half-hour tirade of recrimination
Where, feeling misused, she had got pretty plastered,
And named His name publicly, called him a bastard.
The details are fuzzy, though others have told her
She insulted this one and cried on that shoulder,
Then lurched 'round the ballroom, all pitching and weaving
And ended the night in the ladies' lounge, heaving.

How had it begun, before things all turned rotten?
She can pinpoint the day, she has never forgotten
How he came to her desk and leaned over her chair
To look at some papers, and then smelled her hair.
"Gardenias," he'd said, his voice sultry and lazy
And hot on her ear, Helen felt she'd gone crazy.
"A fragrance so heady it borders on sickly,"
He'd purred at her neck and then just as quickly
Was back to all business, demanding she call
Some client, as if he'd said nothing at all.

She was certainly never an expert at men,
But an inkling was twinkling, especially when
The next day he all but confirmed Helen's hunch.
When he leaned from his office and asked her to lunch.
Their talk was all awkward and formal to start
He said that he found her efficient and smart.
She thanked him, then stopped, she was quite at a loss.

She'd never before really talked to her boss.
They each had martinis, which helped turn things mellow,
He asked where she lived, and if she had a fellow.
He reached for her hand and asked, "Will you allow
An old man to wonder who's kissing you now?"

It was close and convenient, his spare midtown rental.
And after, *more* drinks at a bar near Grand Central
To sit once again in uncomfortable silence
Like two guilty parties to some kind of violence.
They sipped among other oblivion seekers,
While June Christy sang from the bar's tinny speakers.
He settled the bill and they got to their feet,
And emerged from the afternoon hush to the street.

They walked arm in arm in some crude imitation
Of other real couples en route to the station.
Such leisurely strolling, although it's grown late
Against her best judgment it feels like a date.
His booze-cloud blown over, now happy, near beaming
He stops at a window of cutlery, gleaming,
He points out the wares, taking note of a set that
He likes best of all, then he says, "*We* should get that."
She knows it's a joke, all this idle house-playing
But briefly she hopes that he means what he's saying.
Her presence, she thinks, is what's rendered him gladder
But really it's just that he aimed for, and had her.
The hideous reason behind his new glow is
What Helen—and many just like her—don't know is

That men's moods turn light and their spirits expand,
The moment they sense an escape is at hand.
He patted her cheek as he said, "I'm replenished,"
Then off through the crowd for the next train to Greenwich.

Helen pictured his house with its broad flagstone path.
The windows lit up, a child fresh from the bath,
And wondered if *she* might just smell on his skin,
The coppery scent of their afternoon sin.

At her desk the next Monday it was business as always.
There were no words exchanged, not a glance in the hallways.
With relief, Helen thought, *Well that's that. Nevermore.*
'Til Friday (again) at his pied-à-terre door.

And Friday thereafter, and each after that
For close to two years, 'til their actions begat
What such actions are wont to when caution's ignored.
The cure was a thing she could scarcely afford.
They talked in his office behind the closed door.
(She could tell from his face that he'd been there before.)
In the envelope left the next day on her desk,
Was two hundred cash and a downtown address.

She'd never had visions of roses or cupids,
From the beginning she wasn't that stupid.
What you don't hope for can't turn 'round to hurt you.
Besides, she had long before given her virtue.

There hadn't been untoward coaxing or urging
This wasn't The Ogre Defiling The Virgin
He's older than she, but they'd both played the game
Of never once speaking the other one's name.
Their mutual distance a plan jointly hatched
To keep things unserious, flip, and detached.
It was—truth be told, when she coolly reflected—
Not all that much different from what she'd expected.
Expected, she thought, and it sounded absurd.
How long had it been since she'd uttered that word?

And yet there were moments—unbarred, undefended—
When Helen concocted, cooked up, and pretended
She had all the trappings that go with the life of
The thoroughly satisfied, *marrified* wife of
A man who might keep her, despite the new battle
That said wives were really no better than chattel,
The difference too scant between "bridal" and "bridle"
And girls who'd had everything, now suicidal,
Finally finding their voices to speak
Of their feminine fetters, this loathsome mystique;
This problem that theretofore hadn't a name
And still, Helen couldn't resist, just the same,
To wonder, how might such a cared-for existence
Feel after decades of hard-won subsistence.
A mistress of manor, so calm, so serene
To know that there nowhere was any vitrine
Whose silvery wares would be ever denied her.

She tamped such a rampant desire deep inside her
And hoped if she kept the dream hidden and frozen
She soon would forget that she'd never been chosen.

But dreams scream as loud, whether thriving or dying
And Helen despite herself never stopped trying
With boxes of candy to New England camps,
And weekly, she cut and saved all foreign stamps
"I thought that your son . . ." and she'd leave it at that.
He would pocket the packet while donning his hat
And give her a friendly yet cursory nod
In thanks for the postage that came from abroad
With turrets and toucans, or archdukes, and antelope
Carefully trimmed and then slipped in an envelope.
She gave it her all not to trawl for his gaze
And used just those words, thus ensuring the phrase
Stayed tossed off, lest he find her maternal gesture
Too avid, or larded with over-investure.
A strategy subtler than some store-bought toy,
The covert seduction of man through his boy.
And as for less hidden campaigning, that too
Reared its head. Only once, with a "This is for you . . ."
When Helen presented a square of manila,
The contents so personal she thought it might kill her.
And if he suspected her ardor, he'd mock it,
So she was relieved when it joined in the pocket
The stamps. Her relief was compounded still when
He'd never brought up Helen's token again.

The doctor's door must have had five or more locks,
With a sixth to secure Helen's cash in a box.
He lowered the blinds to block out the sun
(Helen felt guilty before they'd begun).
Just a knife-blade of rays now bisected the room,
A useless divider twixt Sorrow and Gloom.
His first words—as though not already quite clear—
Were, "If anyone asks, you have *never* been here."
Helen, to show there would be no such slips,
Turned a key at her mouth as she locked up her lips.
She'd done it to combat the scent of despair
That pervaded the shaded, funereal air,
That she understood and could always be trusted,
But he curled his lip and seemed almost disgusted.
As if she was flirting or being beguiling,
He muttered, "I thought that *by now* you'd stop smiling."
She slackened her face, said "I'm sorry" and hastened
Undressing and feeling quite thoroughly chastened.
She lay back and placed her feet in the cold stirrups
And faced toward the window, all birdsong and chirrups.

A gauzy pad moist with some drops to sedate her,
A red rubber bulb, and a plain kitchen grater
He used on what looked like a brick of pink soap
The color of dawn, the exact shade of hope.
Waxy rose strands fell down into the water
(To flush out a son or incipient daughter?)

Woozy now, Helen regarded the basin
And angled herself so she might put her face in,
and leaned near the surface and took in a breath
Of almonds and ether, of freedom and death.

To help with the nausea, he gave her some pills—
'Though woefully few; she felt green at the gills.
The trip back to Brooklyn, she stood on the train.
She seriously thought she'd pass out from the pain.

———————

There were stories of girls, all summarily sacked, who
Found out they no longer had jobs to come back to,
At least she had that, but she started to feel
That it hardly seemed worth it to work for a heel.
For each passing day found her feeling less grateful
Primarily 'cause he was hurtful and hateful.
Some minimal kindness was not a tall order.
Instead he was rude or he outright ignored her.
Until she decided that this wasn't right.
And stood in the door of his office one night.
She asked if he'd ever again say Hello,
Fedora'd and coated and ready to go
He took a step backward as if sensing danger
And fixed her with eyes of a cold-blooded stranger.
"I don't know what your game is, and frankly don't care,
But don't threaten me, Helen. I warn you, beware."

The very next Monday, from others she heard
That, without her knowledge, he'd had her transferred.
At least (tiny comfort) they didn't demote her
But Helen became what is known as a "floater."
Doing steno for this one, or helping with filing
And through it all Helen made sure to keep smiling.
The salt in the wound was the sight that then faced her,
Those looks he exchanged with the girl who'd replaced her.
She made herself steely, was ever the stoic
She held back her tears with an effort heroic.
But something was growing with each passing day,
'Til it burst forth the night of her shameful display.
She'd figured they'd fire her within the New Year
But Helen soon realized she'd nothing to fear.
(What she didn't know was the company's bosses
Viewed Helen as one of those typical crosses
A company's role it is—sadly—to bear
A lazy one here, or a crazy one there
And so no one made any move to relieve her
But mostly because they just didn't believe her.)

Perhaps there are those who consider it shameful
That Helen comes yearly, all dressed up and gameful.
Just showing herself in the very same setting
Cannot be a help to ensure folks' forgetting.
But she won't stay home or remain out of sight.
To do so, she thinks, *would just prove that they're right.*
She might have been drunk and too forward, uncouth
But each word she'd spoken had been but the truth.

Miss one or two parties and then, before long
The general consensus would be, "She was wrong."
A version to which she refused to be pliant,
So each year, she stands there, alone and defiant
While others quaff cocktails and gradually lose
The strictures that slowly dissolve with the booze.
There's tippling and coupling, embracing with brio.
And all being scored by the hired jazz trio.
Helen just stands there, observing it all,
Sipping her gimlet against the far wall.

The evening progresses, the room now quite loud
And here's Kay from Accounting! She weaves through the
        crowd.
A man on her left arm, a drink in her right.
"All alone are we, Helen? No fella tonight?"
Kay wears on her face an expression of utter
Concern, like her mouth couldn't even melt butter.

And here is the truth Helen long had resisted
In most of their eyes, she just barely existed,
Except as a source of some acid-tinged mirth,
A punch line, it seems, is the source of her worth.
They don't think of that time, indeed, they don't care.
She has always, to them, barely even been there.

The time when this might have been painful is past.
Nothing hurts Helen now, her heart has been cast
In bronze or in iron, or chiseled from lime,

Or some other substance as adamantine.
Her biggest regret is the five wasted years
That she's chided herself over shedding those tears.
Instead of her wishing for eyes that stayed dry
She should cherish that Helen, so able to cry,
That Helen who felt things and then wasn't scared
To air them in public. That Helen who cared
Enough about things she could speak them aloud,
That Helen of whom she might ever be proud.
Taking both of Kay's hands with no rancor, no bile,
Helen looks in her eyes and breaks into a smile.
"You're right," Helen says, "I should call it a day."
Helen smiles one more time, and then adds, "Fuck off, Kay."

Helen takes off her dress and gets ready for bed.
There is peace deep within her, where once only dread.
And there, in the comforting nocturnal gloom
An image took form in the air of her room:
Was it really as distant as sixteen long years
Since Clifford had handed her two golden spheres
He'd plucked from a fruit-laden tangerine tree
And holding his camera had said, "Look at me."
He posed her, half naked, like some Aphrodite.
Helen felt marvelous, brilliant, and mighty
The picture he'd taken was her at her best
The oranges, one each to cover a breast.
She'd never felt better than she did that day

And rued that she'd given the picture away,
She shook her head, pained, for this hardly distinguished
Itself from her many gifts she had relinquished.

She watches the window for most of the night,
Turn from deep black as it gathers up light.
And as the panes bloom to a beautiful blue
She lights on a theory, although it feels true:
Babylonian, Aztec, Gregorian or Julian
All calendars *must* know those hours when cerulean
Skies seem so pure and to go on forever,
That one feels each dream and one's every endeavor's
Success is as sure as the coming of dawn.

She gulped in the air with a satisfied yawn.
A calm had descended around five a.m.,
Which made her immune to the power of Them.
Gets up, quite refreshed, sets the coffee to perk.
For once looking forward to going to work.
She pours out a cup, adds a stream of cold milk
And smiles as it swirls just like taffeta silk.

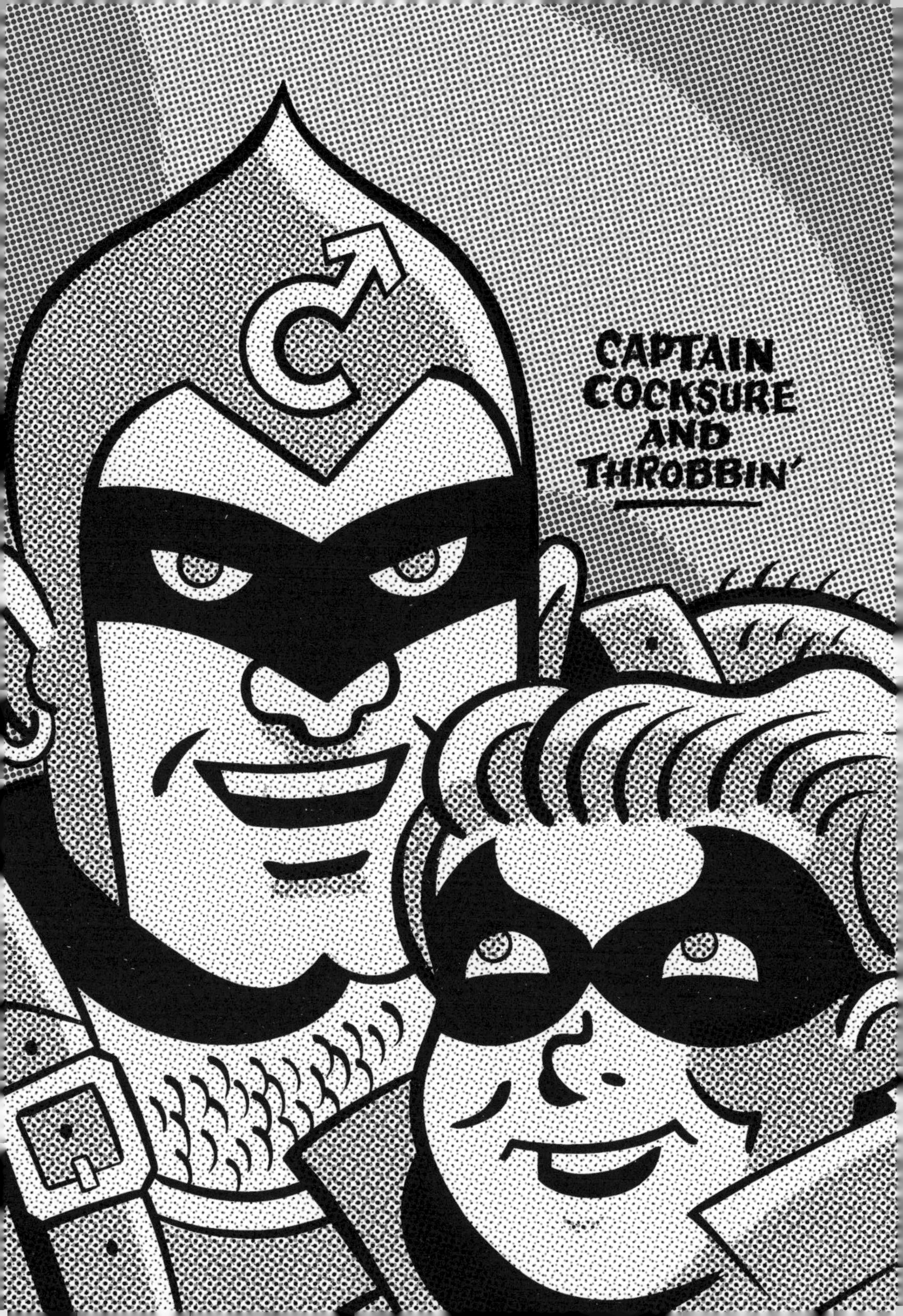
CAPTAIN COCKSURE AND THROBBIN'

O, just like the song says, my heart's San Francisco's!
(Suck on that dear, while I work out where this goes . . .)
From the very first day, Clifford couldn't conceive
Why anyone ever decided to leave.
Hills, Bay, and art, ineluctably bound
To make Clifford feel, *I was lost, now am found*.
And crowning it all was the chief among joys:
The liquid, ubiquitous river of boys.
Fuckable, kissable, dateable, rentable,
Faeries and rough trade, or highly presentable,
Stupid as livestock or literate in Firbank,
All of it galaxies distant from Burbank.

O, San Francisco, I've left you my heart!
(Tug those two down while you rub on that part . . .)
A boy on a stoop who was palming his crotch,
It seemed impolite, Clifford thought, not to watch
Then up to his flat where they diddled for hours,
Another one's rump had near-magical powers;
Clifford the bull and that ass the *torero*
That led him for blocks the wrong way on Guerrero
A mouth like a summer-ripe plum, or a calf
Fuzzed with gold hair, or a neck, or a laugh

Could make Clifford fall (and might leave him with pubic
    lice),
And *still* he felt like he had landed in paradise.

In you, San Francisco, my heart's what I left
(Make your tongue rigid and poke at that cleft . . .)
Smoke a fat spliff and then off to the Castro
Where, blissed-out and bonelessly slumped in the last row
They felt simultaneously boneless and vital
And jazzed by the Wurlitzer's pre-show recital.
Just one more trip taken en masse to the washroom
To have a quick pee and ingest primo mushrooms,
Look at that queen, that unbearable phony
Wearing full leather to Antonioni.
Their thinking was agile, imbued with bravura
Though logic was fragile, so *L'avventura*
Might start out a brilliantly dark meditation
On anomie in the post-war generation
Sick with the bourgeoisie's morals-free habits . . .
Who thinks that the aisles are now crawling with rabbits?
This décor resembles a palace, a mosque, or . . .
How could they deny Judy Garland that Oscar?
It's over with Jimmy, he's petty, aggressive
And frankly, that much *toile* gets pretty oppressive.
Seen *Cabaret*? Liza's three-fourths mascara!
Hey, what was that poem by dear Frank O'Hara?
"Lana Turner get up and . . . shoot John Stompanato!"
My *god*, Kathryn Grayson had killer vibrato.

Wait, Cheryl Whatever was Lana T's daughter
And . . . how have we ended up here at the water?

A quiet walk home, maybe rent a blue video
The velvet-black woods of the nighttime Presidio
Tempered the high's non-contextual mirth
And slowly returned them to heaven on earth.
The wee small hours always concluded with this
A feeling of grateful repletion and bliss.
He thought to himself, "How pear-shaped could this go
Anywhere *other* than my San Francisco."
An insight that always cut keen as a knife
Whose wound was pure pleasure; Clifford loved, *loved* his
    life.
And credited most of that to his dear city,
He lived the reverse of what plagued Walter Mitty
No secrets, no longing, no desperate hoping
Just reach out and grab from a world cracked wide open.

———————

Clifford once hoped that each Bay Area Brahmin
Would, aside from their wealth, have one more thing in
    common:
A portrait by him, rich with painterly skill,
He'd soon be the Sargent—nowadays—of Nob Hill
But that dream was forced through a major revision
The *instant* he'd gone out to drum up commissions.

Fresh out of art school, and more than proficient
He'd thought, like a dope, that his gifts were sufficient.
Not understanding his role was a mixture
Of lapdog and popinjay, servant and fixture.
Cliff lacked the fawning gene, just couldn't glom
Onto dowagers ignorant of Vietnam,
Or husbands who thought it was his first time hearing
The usual jokes about "guys who have earrings."
"I thought you were some chick, with all that long hair."
(Although a true passion of his, somehow the ratio
Was off; Clifford just could not give that much fellatio.)
The only regret was one of economics
When he quit for a life in the underground comics.
But the joy of it outshone his bank account's lack,
He climbed down from Nob Hill and never looked back.

––––––––––

Who left their heart in San Fran? It was me!
(It's so good with two, dear. Shall we try three?)
Body surf over the ocean's green swells,
Truffle for dick or go forage morels.
Sun-washed and fog-bound, electric with sex
Challenging, easy, naïve, and complex
It *still* filled him with a near-supplicant awe
That even grown up, they allowed him to draw
And then—here's the part that was screamingly funny—
They'd then say "Good job, Cliff," and then give him money!

Be a go-getter or bonelessly languid,
Laid out, displayed like a groaning-board banquet.
The square and the dyke and the faggot, the freak
Could easily find and then get what they seek
Unlike, say, New York where, regardless of hope
Or desire, lay a point where a red velvet rope
Stood between you and the goals of your dreams
(At least when he visits, that's just how it seems).

"Cap'n Cocksure and Throbbin'," his randy young pal
In tales like "The Shoot-out at KY Corral."
Regardless of each issue's sticky predicaments
They'd end in a blending of muscles and ligaments.
He brought to bear all from his life-drawing class
(Plus, given the Cap'n his ex's Pete's ass).
Tights of carnelian, a jock blue as lapis
And filled to a size as befitting Priapus.
In truth, he was Bruce Wang, a wealthy civilian
(The jokes were all similarly crude and vaudevillian).
Monthly, he'd battle some muscular villain
Who turned almost instantly horny and willing,
And ended with Cap'n who'd then throw his massive . . .
Err . . . *weight* behind Throbbin', posed Grecian (and
        passive).
Thrusting and pumping, reliably nude,
Cliff's magnum opus was thrillingly lewd.
The work of an overgrown, over-sexed kid
Rex Bond unfiltered, by way of Cliff's id.

Blanche Tilley believed in true Heaven, real Hell
Her hair an immovable nautilus shell,
Was galvanized with a conviction near feral
When she sensed that children were somehow in peril.
Unburdened by much intellectual heft
She battled the evil she saw on the Left
"A mere servant to all concerned wives and mothers."
(A woman who, truthfully, given her druthers,
Would see all the Libbers, the Hippies, the Gays
Hounded and rounded up and locked away.)
"I look at the state of this country today
And see such depravity, moral decay
That, truly, it makes me just weep for the nation
These crimes in the name of their 'Gay Liberation.'
Just how do the First Amendment's full rights
Extend to this sodomite rapist in tights?"
She called the strip filthy, overt, immature.
All charges to which Cliff responded with "Sure!
Cocksure is vulgar, he's dirty and loud
Excessive and horny, and makes me so proud.
I draw him for those who might like it or need it,
But if you don't want to, Blanche, well, then don't read it!

"In some ways we two are a heaven-made match
But like much in life, there's a deal-breaking catch:
We both love our lives, our convictions are strong
You'd think we'd be fast friends, but you would think wrong.
We think *we're* the ones who are open, convivial
While others are hateful if not downright trivial.

We each fill the other with loathing and fear
We'd each like the other to just disappear.
To you, I'm a sinner, sprung full-formed from Sodom
Of lowliest creatures, I dwell at the bottom
I know it won't sway you the smallest scintilla
To point out the sex is quite firmly vanilla,
The hatred you harbor's divorced from reality
I draw a sweet blow job, you see bestiality.
How I wish you would stop up that bile-spewing spigot
You use when you speak, you rebarbative bigot.
You're through and through Dixie and I, San Francisco.
Despite a shared fondness we both have for Crisco,
Try as I might, I simply can't see
A way or a day when we two might agree.
So pack up your sideshow and go back down South
Where I won't come knock the dick out of *your* mouth."

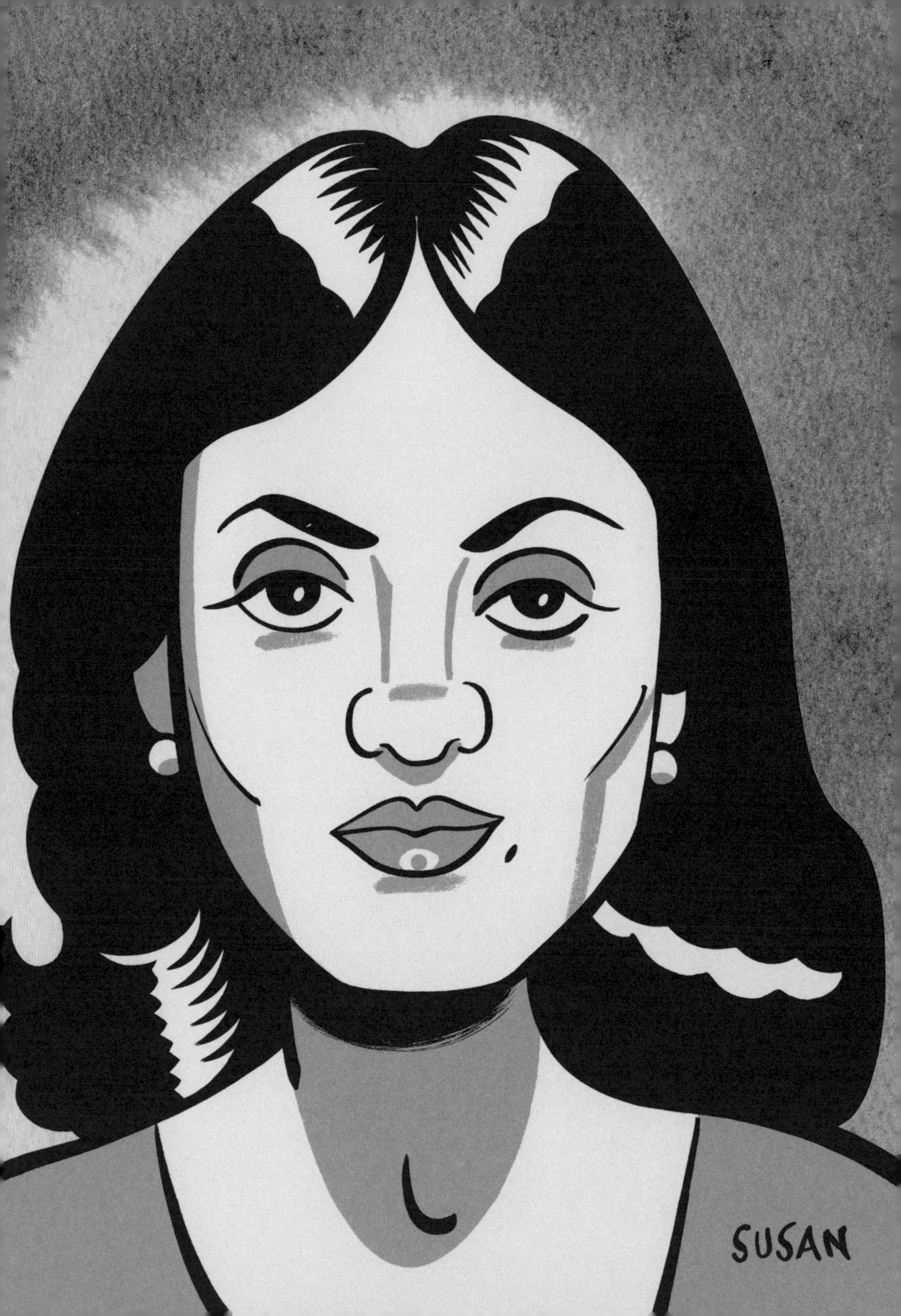
SUSAN

Susan had never donned quite so bourgeois
A garment as Thursday night's Christian Lacroix.
In college—just five years gone—she'd have abhorred it
But now, being honest, she fucking adored it.
The shoulders, the bodice, *insane* retro pouf,
Where once an indictment, now good, calming proof;
She'd no longer be tarred by the words "shame" or "greed,"
Tossed about by the weak. No, now Susan was freed!
If she wanted to spend half the whole day adorning
Herself, well what of it? The American Morning
Had dawned! At Oberlin stuff she'd feigned being above,
Had turned into all that she most dearly loved.
And conversely, stuff she might actively seek
Now repelled her as sub-par, too lenient, and weak.
Out was group therapy (adieu agoraphobics!),
In was massage, Silver Palate, aerobics.
Innermost was a Susan Improved and Untrammeled
Sleeker and diamond-bright, sharp and enameled!
She happily ate "poisonous" white-flour pasta
Whereas all those Ultimate Frisbee white Rastas
Didn't seem sexy and free anymore,
And frankly, the U.S. in El Salvador
(Or out of it? Truly, she'd largely lost track
And hadn't the patience to find her way back),

Among frailer aspects of the human condition
Now just turned her stomach. Once-hated ambition
Awakened her senses like rarest perfume;
It could render her weak-kneed across a large room.

It was all large rooms lately, all beautifully appointed
And Susan had somehow been specially anointed
To stand in them prettily, playing her part:
Girl at the nexus of commerce and art.
Her father was glad to augment the small salary
She made as factotum at the Nonnie Cash Gallery.
Nonnie was in the news seven months back
When she'd ended a group show by handing out crack.
"Let's turn this new vice into something convivial!"
(The chief of police called her "clueless and trivial.")
Susan adored her and worshipped her style,
Loved her pronouncements of "perfect" and "vile,"
Loved the sheer whim, the madcap willy-nillyness
And how deeply seriously Nonnie took her own silliness
(Though she'd have loved Hitler, if forced to confess,
If he had seen fit to have bought her that dress).

"The opening demands it!" Nonnie said on their spree,
"And Spraycan can bloody well pay, thanks to me."
There was bourbon in hypos, doled out by chic nurses—
in truth white-clad models—Osetra beggars' purses.
The waiters were done up like Jean Genet felons:
Brush-cuts, fake shiners, with asses like melons.
And serving as Boswells to Nonnie's new caper,

Scribes from *East Village Eye*, *FMR*, *Paper*.
Nonnie barked orders in Urdu and Xhosa,
And with a *"Ragazzi, servite qualcosa!"*
Came the blush that rose when her blood started to sing
From a room where the energy gets into swing.
Look at this shit, she thought, *pure onanism!*
Ransom-note lettering, sequins, and jism,
Neiman impasto with touches of Basquiat,
Smoke, sizzle, bells, whistles . . . all of it diddly-squat!
Nonnie'd built him a name by dint of sheer will.
A bluff that distracted from his lack of skill.
Despite what collectors seemed willing to pay,
Spraycan 3000 had nothing to say.

Nathan was due as the evening wound down.
They'd rented a car for a week out of town.
Josh was in Chappaqua seeing his mom
They'd stop, pick him up, then continue right on
With luck they would reach the Cape not long past one,
A week on the ocean had sounded like fun.
But then the foreboding that started to loom
When Susan saw Nate standing there 'cross the room,
Clad in the uniform he'd worn since Ohio:
Birkenstocks, drawstring pants (think Putumayo).
With no small remorse, she thought, *He and his mess*
Better not come near this fabulous dress.

———

Ah, whither love's ardor whose heat used to scorch her?
Now his mere face can assail her like torture
And being alone with him renders her frantic
It makes her a hectoring shrew, a pedantic
Wet blanket, although it is *also* true, in her defense
That Nate can be maddeningly oafish and dense.
Who chips a mug without knowing it, or
Doesn't see that they've just spilt some milk on the floor?
And once pointed out, he goes all Lotus
Position-y, saying mildly, "Wow. I didn't notice."
She didn't want some belching, farting, or toga-
Clad frat boy, but frankly, the wheat germ, the yoga
Seemed ersatz, some also-ran version of "mellow,"
This go-with-the-flow, unassailable fellow,
She just didn't buy Nathan's pressure-wrought grace,
And wanted sometimes just to slap that sweet face.

Now Day Three in Wellfleet, they've lost all their power
Which means no hot water, no lights, and cold showers.
And all Nathan does is repeat "This is cozy."
She thinks that perhaps she'll just get up and mosey
To where he is sitting to give him a smack.
Maybe the blow would do something to crack
This passive-aggressive façade for his shirking
Just going downstairs to get things back to working.
Or maybe, she thinks, *I'll just fuck your best friend.*
Now, something like that might just bring to an end
This constant pretending that everything's fine.
Maybe then you might evidence some sort of spine.

A thunderstorm could be heard off in the distance.
Susan had offered Josh any assistance.
"Sure," Josh replied, "you can come hold the ladder."
Nathan kept reading, which just made her madder,
And then madder *still* when he hadn't detected
Her tone, which was heavily sarcasm-inflected:
"Need anything up here, Nate, before we're done?"
"No, that's okay," Nate replied, "you guys have fun."
"We will." Her smile had a slight rodentine tightness.
Nathan went back to his *Unbearable Lightness*
Of Being, that summer's one de rigueur book,
And, lost in the story, did not even look
Up from the page for an hour or more
When the others came through the basement stairs door.
"You were gone for a while. Must have got a lot done."
"Oh, we did," Susan said, squinting, as the lights all
       surged on.

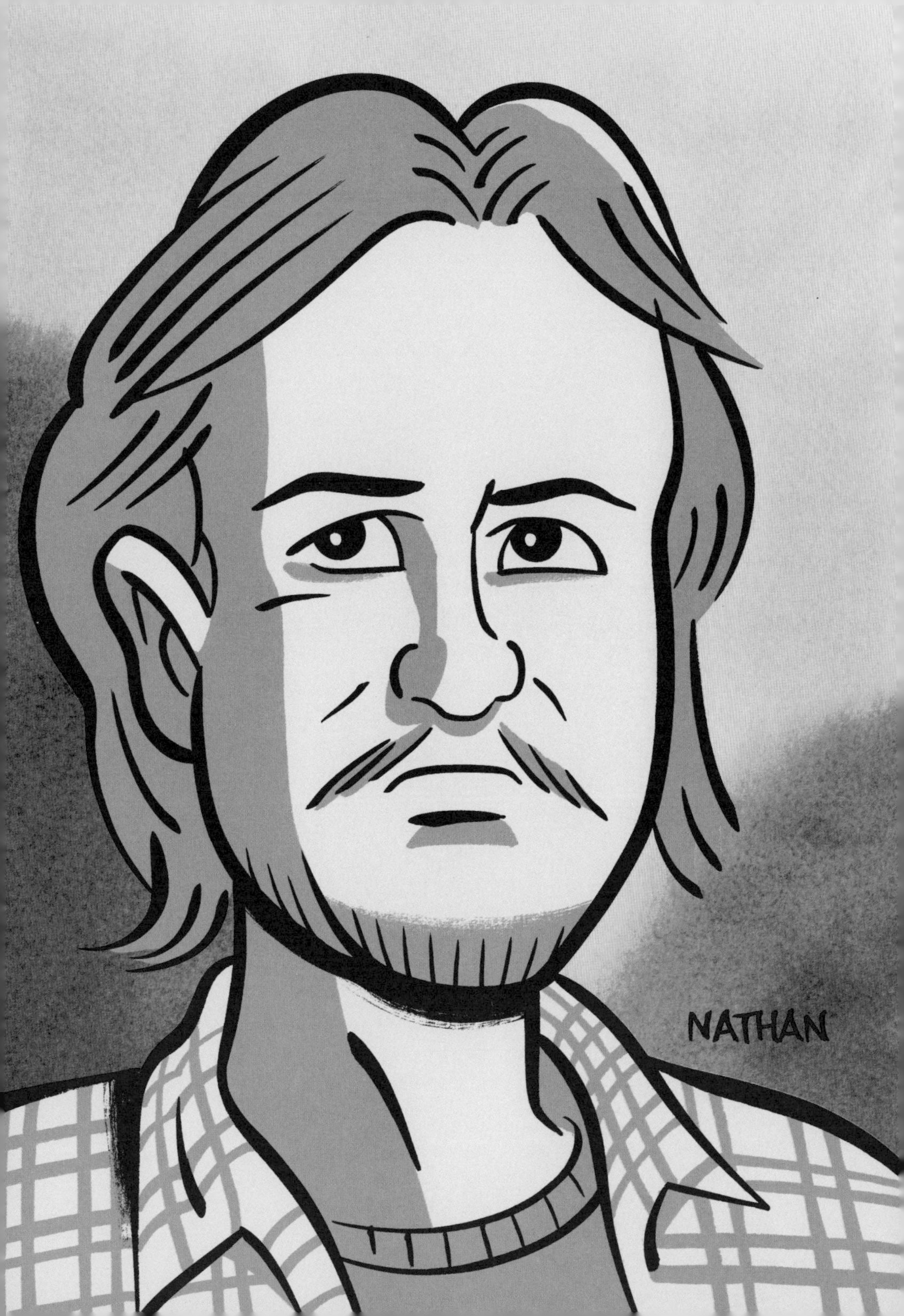
NATHAN

Take Posner's of Great Neck, the Falls at Niagara
And throw in that white marble tomb that's in Agra—
Now if you compared the three places, you might
Think the Taj and Niagara were hiding their light.
At Posner's, the subtle, subdued, and hermetic
Had no part to play. The rococo aesthetic—
An Empire, Art Deco, Chinoiserie garble
Of crystal and frescoes and gilt and (yes) marble;
A maximal, turbo-charged, top-drawer milieu—
Appealed to a moneyed crowd of locals who
Insisted on only the toppest of drawers,
Weddings befitting a Louis Quatorze.
Venetian palazzo floors pounded by horas
Cut-velvet drapes framing chopped-liver Torahs.
Ceilings adorned with Tiepolo clouds
Vaulted above the dressed-to-the-nines crowds
Who gave off their *own* light with such glinting frequency
(good thing one need not kill creatures for sequins).

Nathan, from one of the outlying tables,
His feet tangled up in the disc jockey's cables,
Surveyed the room as unseen as a ghost
While he mulled over what he might say for his toast.

That the couple had asked him for this benediction
Seemed at odds with them parking him here by the kitchen.
His invite was late—a forgotten addendum—
For Nate, there could be no more clear referendum
That he need but endure through this evening and then
He would likely not see Josh and Susan again.

That he had said yes was still a surprise,
And not just to him, it was there in the eyes
Of the guests who had seen a mirage and drew near
And then covered their shock with a "Nathan, you're here!"
And then silence, they'd nothing to say beyond that.
A few of the braver souls lingered to chat
They all knew, it was neither a secret nor mystery
That he and the couple had quite an odd history
Their bonds were a tangle of friendship and sex.
Josh his best pal once, and Susan his ex.
For a while he could hardly go out in the city
Without being a punch line or object of pity.
"Poor Nathan" had virtually become his real name
And so he showed up just to show he was game.
His shirt had been ironed, his belt brightly buckled,
A shine on his shoes, a well-turned-out cuckold.

Susan's sister was speaking, a princess in peach.
"Hello, I am Mindy, and this is my speech.
Susan, you are the best sister plus you've always had great comic
timing,

So I know you won't hold it against me when I do my specialty
    and

                                make my toast in rhyming.
You've always been a terrific runner, even though it made your
    shoes damp
Especially when you were impersonating Mrs. Zolteck from Tal-
    mud Torah

                               when we were at camp.
Josh, we have become the best of friends and I'm so happy now I'm
    your sister,
But when we go out together let's try not to get blisters . . ."

Nathan's mind wandered as Mindy meandered.
The effort he'd squandered, if this was the standard,
Seemed hours badly wasted, until he recalled
That, time notwithstanding, he'd nothing at all.
He'd pored over *Bartlett's* for couplets to filch
He'd stayed up 'til three and still came up with zilch
Except for instructions he'd underscored twice
Just two words in length, and those words were,
    "Be Nice!"
Too often, he'd noticed, emotions betray us
And reason departs once we're up on the dais.
He'd witnessed uncomfortable moments where others
Had lost their way quickly, where sisters and brothers
Had gotten too prickly and peppered their babbling
With stories of benders or lesbian dabbling,
Or spot-on impressions of mothers-in-law,

Which, true, Nathan thought, always garnered guffaws
But the price seemed too high with the laughs seldom
    cloaking
Hostility masquerading as joking.

No, he'd swallow his rage and bank all his fire
He knew that in his case the bar was set higher.
He'd have to be careful and hide what his heart meant
(Disingenuous malice was Susan's department).
They'd be hungry for blood even though they had supped,
Folks were just waiting for him to erupt
In tears or some other unsightly reaction,
And Nathan would not give them that satisfaction.
Though Susan's a slattern, and Josh was a lout
At least Nathan knew what he'd *not* talk about:

I won't wish them divorce, that they wither and sicken,
Or tonight that they choke on their salmon (or chicken).
I'll stay mum on that time when the cottage lost power
In that storm on the Cape, and they left for an hour
And they thought it was just the cleverest ruse
To pretend it took that long to switch out the fuse.
Or that time you advised me, with so much insistence,
That I should be granting poor Susan more distance.
That the worst I could do was to hamper and crowd her,
That if she felt stifled she'd just take a powder.
That a plant needs its space just as much as its water
And above all, not give her the ring that I'd bought her.

Which in retrospect only elicits a "Gosh!
I hardly deserved a friend like you, Josh."

No, I won't air that laundry, or make myself foolish
To satisfy appetites venal and ghoulish.
I will *not* be the blot on this hellish affair.
And with that Nathan pushed out, and rose from his chair.
And just by the tapping of knife against crystal,
All eyes turned his way, like he'd fired off a pistol.

"Joshua, Susan, dear family and friends,
A few words, if you will, before everything ends
And you skip out of here to begin your new life
As happily married husband and wife.
You've promised to honor, to love and obey,
We've sipped our champagne and been cleansed with sorbet
All in endorsement of your Hers and His-dom.
So, let me add my two cents' worth of wisdom.
Herewith, as a coda to this evening historical
I just thought I'd tell you this tale allegorical.

I was wracking my brains sitting here at this table
Until I remembered this suitable fable.
Each reptilian hero, each animal squeal
Serves a purpose, you see, because they reveal
A truth about life, even as they distort us
So here is 'The Tale of the Scorpion and Tortoise.'

The scorpion was hamstrung, his tail all aquiver.
Just how would he manage to get 'cross the river?
'The water's so deep,' he observed with a sigh,
Which pricked at the ears of the tortoise nearby.
'Well, why don't you swim?' asked the slow-moving fellow.
'Unless you're afraid. Is that it, you are yellow?'
'That's rude,' said the scorpion, 'and I'm not afraid
So much as unable. It's not how I'm made.'

'Forgive me, I didn't mean to be glib when
I said that, I figured you were an amphibian.
The error was one of misclassification
I mistakenly figured you for a crustacean.'

'No offense taken,' the scorpion replied.
'But how 'bout you help me to reach the far side?
You swim like a dream, and you have what I lack.
What say you take me across on your back?'

'I'm really not sure that's the best thing to do,'
Said the tortoise, 'Now that I see that it's you.
You're the scorpion and—how can I say this?—just . . . well . . .
I don't know I feel safe with you riding my shell.
You've a less-than-ideal reputation preceding.
There's talk of your victims, all poisoned and bleeding,
That fact by itself should be reason sufficient.
I mean, what do you take me for, mentally deficient?'

'I hear what you're saying, but what would that prove?
We'd both drown so tell me, how would that behoove
Me, to basically die at my very own hand
When all I desire is to be on dry land?'

The tortoise considered the scorpion's defense.
When he gave it some thought, it made perfect sense.
The niggling voice in his mind he ignored
And he swam to the bank and called out 'Climb aboard.'

The tortoise was wrong to ignore all his doubts
Because in the end, friends, our true selves will out.
For, just a few moments from when they set sail
The scorpion lashed out with his venomous tail.
The tortoise, too late, understood that he'd blundered
When he felt his flesh stabbed and his carapace sundered.
As he fought for his life, he said, 'Please tell me why
You have done this, for now we will surely both die!'

'I don't know,' cried the scorpion. 'You never should trust
A creature like me, because poison I must.
I'd claim some remorse or at least some compunction
But I just can't help it. My form is my function.
You thought I'd behave like my cousin the crab
But unlike him, it is but my *nature* to stab.'

The tortoise expired with one final quiver
And then both of them sank, swallowed up by the river."

Nathan paused, cleared his throat, took a sip of his drink.
He needed these extra few seconds to think.
The room had grown frosty, the tension was growing,
Folks wondered precisely where Nathan was going.
The prospects of skirting fiasco seemed dim
But what he said next surprised even him.

"So what can we learn from their watery ends?
Is there some lesson on how to be friends?
I think what it means is that central to living
A life that is good is a life that's forgiving.
We're creatures of contact, regardless of whether
to kiss or to wound, we still must come together.
Like in *Annie Hall*, we endure twists and torsions
For food we don't like, and in such tiny portions!
But, like hating a food but still asking for more
It beats staying dry but so lonely on shore.
So we make ourselves open, while knowing full well
It's essentially saying, 'Please, come pierce my shell.'
So . . . please, let's all raise up our glasses of wine
And I'll finish this toast with these words that aren't mine:
Yet each man kills the thing he loves,
By each let this be heard,
Some do it with a bitter look,
Some with a flattering word,
The coward does it with a kiss,
The brave man with a sword!"

Where first it seemed that Nathan had his old resentments
    cleanly hurdled,
The air now held the mildest scent of something sweet gone
    meanly curdled.
The thorough ambiguity held guests in states of mild
    confusion
No one raised their eyes, lest a met glance be taken for
    collusion.
Silence doesn't paint the depth of quiet in that room
There was no clinking stemware toasting to the bride or
    groom.
You could have heard a petal as it landed on the floor.
And in that quiet Nathan turned and walked right out the
    door.

The urinal's wall was *The King and His Court*,
A work done in porcelain, precisely the sort
Of tableau of gentility at Le Petit Trianon,
A cast of nobility, designed for the peeing on.
Nate turned his gaze as he hosed down the scene,
It seemed an especially brutish and mean
Treatment of all the baroque figures in it
(Such unlucky placement, poor girl at her spinet).
He needed this pit stop before he took off
To go catch his train, when he heard a slight cough.

There, twisting a swan's head in gold for hot water
Was Lou, who had bankrolled this day for his daughter.

Lou had scared Nathan for all of the years
He was with Susan, and now the sum of his fears
Was here, now the chickens had come home to land.
"The man of the hour, with his *schvantz* in his hand."
Nathan started to say that he knew how he blew it
And how he was sorry, but Lou beat him to it;
Lou, who was blunt—some said boorish—and rich.
But a mensch deep at heart, said, "My Suzy's a bitch.
You'd think that today I'd be proud, that I'd *kvell*,
But I followed you out here just so I could tell
You: she told her friends she would be able to get
You to come give a toast. It's a monstrous bet,
Made all the more awful that her Day of Joy
Was *still* incomplete, and abusing a boy
In a trick was the thing that she wanted above
All else. It's the mark of a girl who can't love.
Ach, Nathan, this day is a stroke of bad luck.
You, cast in this play, and then played for a schmuck.
But think of it this way, she'll wake up tomorrow
And *still* be unhappy. And that is *my* sorrow."

Lou turned off the swan's head, once more checked his tie,
Held his arm out and said, "This is good-bye."
He shook Nathan's hand and then made for the door
Where he paused and he turned to say just one thing more.
"That toast, if you give it again (but you won't),
Remember, Nate: turtles swim, tortoises don't."

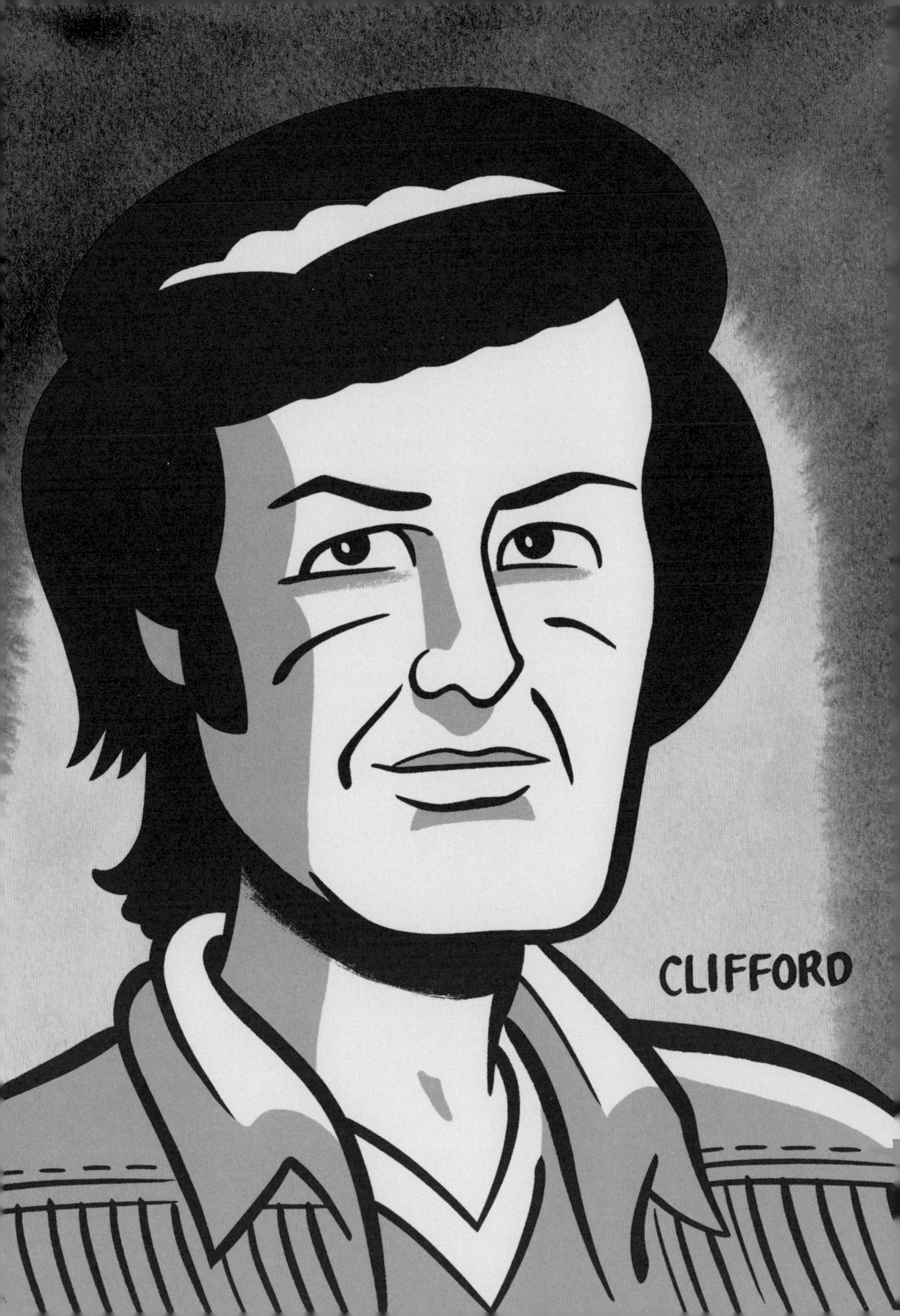
CLIFFORD

A permeable world where each friend is a trick,
Can feel like it's crumbling when just one gets sick.
Add one more for two, and that queasy sensation
Can feel like a threat to one's very foundation.
Three seems like carelessness, a surfeit of strife
Exposing one to comment on the Platform of Life
(Yes, dear Lady Bracknell, invoked with remorse
But humor was Cliff's one remaining recourse);
For if "sick" becomes "die" and then "three," "*every* friend,"
It's the hurricane's eye of a world at an end,
A Vale of Tears reached 'cross a sad Bridge of Sighs,
Cliff and his cohort were dropping like flies:

Victor, a handsome star of the ballet
Whose turnout, they said, could turn anyone gay
Coughed once, and then he expired like Camille—
Not quite, but the true facts seemed just as surreal—
And what could one say about poor lovely Marty?
Whose fever spiked high at his own dinner party
Between the clear soup and the rabbit terrine
By eleven that night, he was in quarantine.
Marco was the anchor of *Bay Area News Day*.
Fevered on Friday and dead the next Tuesday.
Gorgeous and baritone, gifted with words

And felled by an illness that struck only birds.
Before all they'd had to look out for was crabs
But now nothing helped, there were no pills, no labs
Nothing to slow down, never mind getting rid
Of this crazy-fast killer they'd weakly named GRID.

A grid: Cliff could see it stretched out, made of wire,
And spanning a canyon of brimstone and fire.
Suddenly, all of them caught unawares
Were one by one falling away through its squares
Rampant infections called opportunistic
Worked at a pace both absurd and sadistic.

The plum-colored smudge, a sloe slowly blooming,
Seemed barely worth noticing; small, unassuming,
As if trying to belie all the terrible harm it
Could do, it stayed hidden, just under his armpit.
But soon it branched out, making siblings and cousins
His lesions were legion, from just one to dozens.
Despite all his nursing, the tears and the dramas
Of friends, when he woke up to find his pajamas
As wet through with sweat as if dunked in the sea
He *still* briefly asked, *What is happening to me?*
He'd loved *Touch of Evil*, when la Dietrich tells
The fortune of corpulent, vile Orson Welles:
"Your future's all used up." So funny and grim.
But now that the same could be spoken of him
It was sadness that gripped him, far more than the fear
That, if facing the truth, he had maybe a year.

When poetic phrases like "eyes, look your last"
Become true, all you want is to stay, to hold fast.
A new, fierce attachment to all of this world
Now pierced him, it stabbed like a deity-hurled
Lightning bolt lancing him, sent from above,
Left him giddy and tearful. It felt like young love.
He'd thought of himself as uniquely proficient
At seeing, but now that sense felt insufficient.
He wanted to grab, to possess, to devour
To *eat* with his eyes, how he needed that power.

Not much of a joiner, he'd always been leery
Of groups, although now, he was simply too weary
From all of the death, plus his symptoms now besting
Him. He so admired those heroes protesting
The drugmakers, government—all who'd forsaken
The thousands—the murderous silence of Reagan,
Or William F. Buckley, that fucker at whose
Suggestion that people with AIDS get tattoos;
(The New Haven lockjaw, the glib erudition,
When truly, the man's craven moral perdition
Made Clifford so angry he thought he might vomit
Or fly east, find Buckley's address, and then bomb it).

But, just like a child whose big gun is a stick,
Cliff was now harmless, he'd gotten too sick
To take any action beyond rudimentary
Routines that had shrunk to the most elementary:
Which pill to take now, and where is your sweater?

Did the Imodium make you feel better?
Study your shit to make sure you'd not bled,
Make sure the Kleenex is next to the bed.
"Make sure," "be prepared," plan out every endeavor
Like a scout on the stupidest camping trip ever.
The facts were now harder, reality colder
His parasol no match for that falling boulder.
And so the concern with the trivial issues:
Slippers nearby and the proximate tissues
He thought of those two things in life that don't vary
(Well, thought only glancingly; more was too scary)
Inevitable, why even bother to test it,
He'd paid all his taxes, so that left . . . you guessed it.

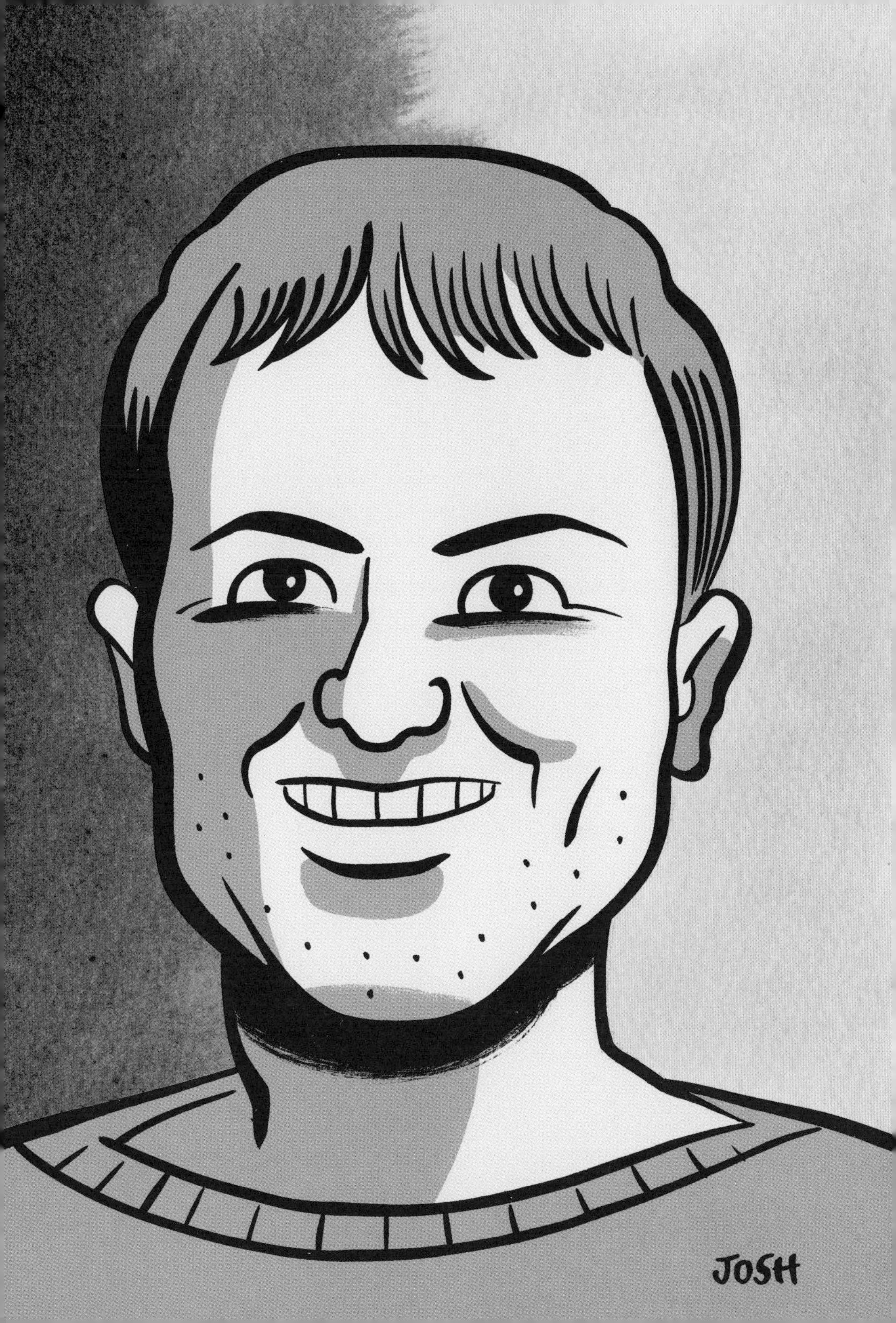
JOSH

Suppose one were trying to gently assert
One's position; an East Eighty-third Street address doesn't
    hurt.
Nor does a cottage on Georgica Pond,
Or three (Jewish . . . *shah!*) kids who are natural blonds.
Susan had banished all unsightly elements
Her latest career would brook no such impediment
To being the personal, shining reflection
Of breeding and privilege, class and connection.
Finally, to match Mayflower Realty, Inc.'s tone
Her business cards now showed her first name as Sloan.

Josh was a force of the courts—law and squash—
The family was blessed and seemed wholly awash
In the kind of good fortune one doesn't dare dream,
Near-parodically copious, bursting the seams
Of the sky; heaven-sent, like the biblical gift of the manna,
Until her thoughts happened to land upon Hannah.
One Hannah Hint seems to be all that it takes
For Sloan's inner Lexus to slam on the brakes.
Her mind gave a lurch, and Hannah's place in it
Was *poof!* purged and cleansed in just under a minute.

Instead, she corralled her thoughts only to roam
On things bright and lovely. For instance, her home:
Everything perfect, divine, and appealing,
The pearl-gray luster of the silver-leafed ceiling
Tamed what most rooms might not easily handle,
Tassels and chintzes, a screen (coromandel),
Sofas and slipper chairs, two silk *fauteuils*
(out of bounds to her girl and both the boys),
Framed scenes of hunts on a hunter-green wall,
A pillow: "Nouveau riche beats no riche at all,"
Traces of Oberlin, NPR, grunge
Gone, and instead was a WASP-y mélange
Of faux Sister Parish, Buatta, and Trump,
A richness of embarrassments, an opulent sump.

Every time Sloan sipped her tea there, *Hosanna*
She thought, *I've arrived* and then . . . Hannah.
(It drove Sloan bananas how seldom, if ever,
The shit of life didn't demolish her reverie.)
She knew it was harsh of her, bordering on churlish—
She tried, in all things, to seem dainty and girlish—
But her mother-in-law made her furious and sick,
Hannah's decline seemed a purposeful trick
Designed to wreak havoc, annoy, to be grating
And, at the worst moments, just plain nauseating.
Once, during a party—this was early on—
Sloan looked around when she noticed her gone.
The very next moment, the elevator attendant
Was at the front door with a Hannah resplendent

Her skirt 'round her shoulders, like the cape of a matador,
Nude and soiled from the waist down, and *walking the
     corridor!*

Josh took his mother straight off to the bath,
While Sloan tried her best to conceal the white wrath
That shot through her with such force she thought she might
     faint,
Especially when friends whispered, "Josh is a saint."
"Yes," she joked, "just the kind I'd like to martyr."
Okay, charade over! It was time now to cart her
Away. She was no longer fit even to visit.
(That's not the mark of a bad person, is it?)

She felt for Josh, truly. He'd grown up with no father,
But Hannah was now such an unruly bother
That Sloan was quite worried that she'd grow to hate him,
Or soon might resort to some harsh ultimatum
Like "It's her or me!" or the wholesale preempting
Of contact, although it grew ever more tempting
(Her feelings for Hannah, alas, were too late;
That vaginal vernissage had sealed her fate).
Each time she even attempted to air
The topic with Josh, his face was despair
Writ so large, deep, and painful she'd had to leave off
(She'd not known she'd married a man quite so soft).
And then, the true kicker: *Could this be prophetic?*
I've read that dementia like this is genetic.

She thought of the joke she and Josh used to tell,
Although it fit present conditions too well:
"If all of the money was gone from my life,
Would you still love me?" a man asks his wife.
"Of course," she replies. "Come here, let me kiss you.
I'll love you forever, but *boy* would I miss you!"

Enough! There was work to do, one saving grace;
She felt the old thrill of a three-agent race
For the exclusive on an absolute jewel:
Four-bedroom penthouse, two fireplaces, *pool*!
And three thousand square feet of wraparound terrace.
Now that's what we need, she thought, feeling embarrassed.
She had windows aplenty, but why shut themselves
Up like corpses on one of those mortuary shelves?
Josh might even bid, if she skillfully seeded
The ground, somehow showing that what they both needed
Was some sort of shake-up, a change of the scenery,
Somewhere to swim, with salubrious greenery,
A respite of peace from the scourge of Alzheimer's
And no one could ever dismiss them as climbers.
She'd get there, but 'til then, she knew it would haunt
Her. *That's good. It means one's alive to still want.*

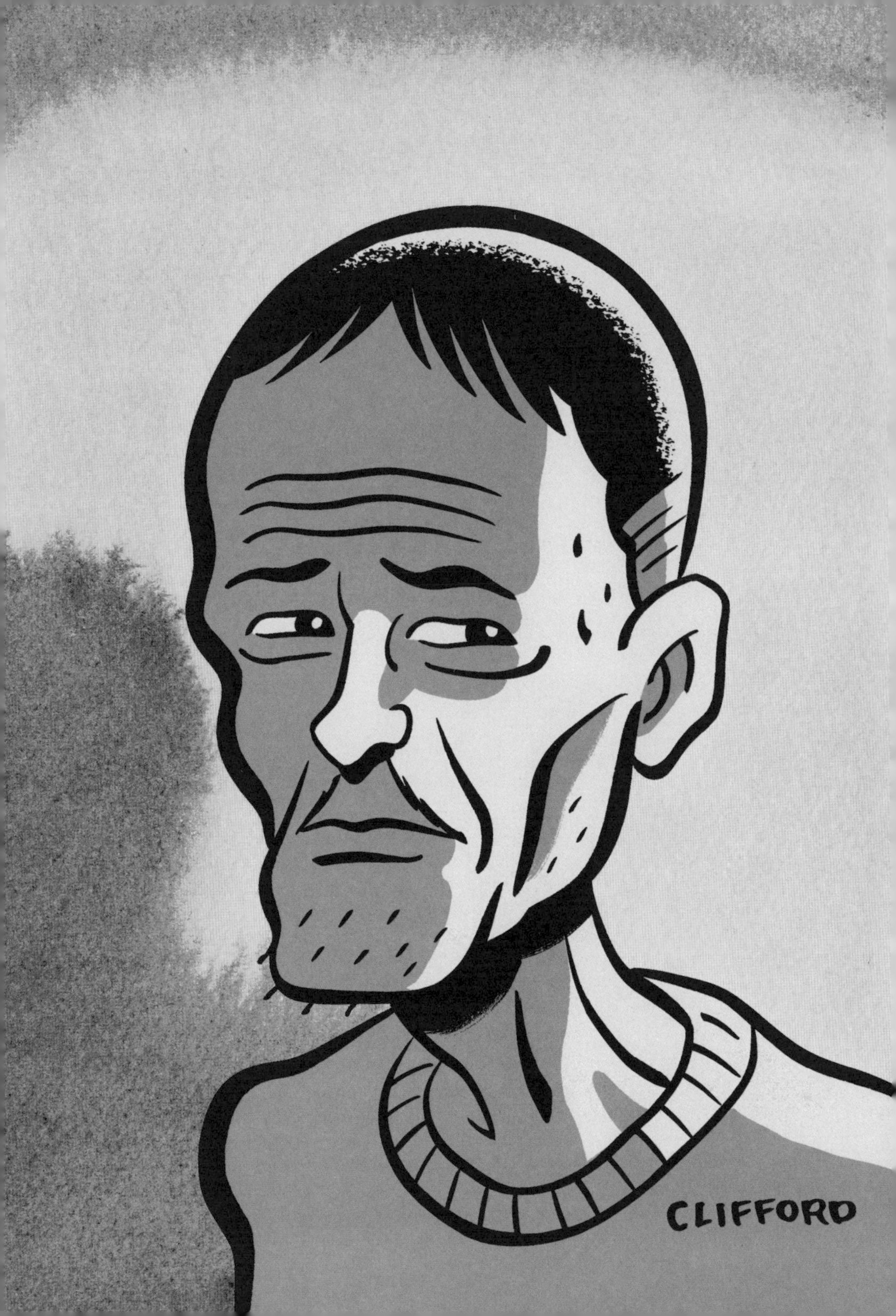
CLIFFORD

What a difference a day makes. Now times that by twenty.
Clifford was hollow, a Horn of Un-Plenty.
Tipping the scales at one-fifteen at most
He was more bone than flesh now, and less man than ghost.
The CMV daily lay waste to his sight
Now, it was all Renoir smearings of light,
I loathe Renoir, Clifford thought, *chocolate-box hack*.
Chuckling, his hacking cough wrenching his back.
"Renoir is chocolate," he said, the words hazy.
Luis, his health aide, laughed: "Cliffie, you're crazy!"
Luis was bull-strong, endlessly calm and
Had magic hands: always cool, smelling of almonds.
Luis, in place of dead parents, friends, lovers,
Rubbed Clifford's temples and tucked in the covers.

High noon, and yet the light steadily dimming,
Beautiful Schubert's trout beautifully swimming.
Half-thoughts and memories swam through his brain:
Glass-soled shoes, Burbank, a berth on a train;
Sally, who'd taught him to make a martini,
The silk jacquard robe on the Doge by Bellini,
Helen! With mandarins shielding her breasts,
Of all his life's work, this one image was best.

His father, among the most gentle of men,
The powdery scent of geraniums, and then . . .

The inkwell tipped over and spread 'cross his page.
Clifford was gone. Forty-five years of age.

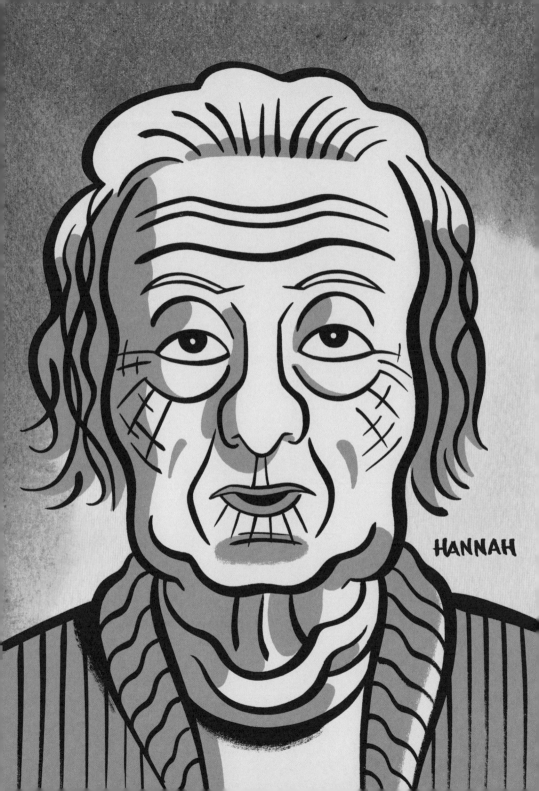
HANNAH

"You look like my Josh, only handsome," she'd say.
She said or did one heartbreaking thing every day.
If Tuesday's mere hygiene was markedly worse,
By Wednesday she'd Homerically re-named her nurse
"that cunt who is stealing right out of my purse."
Like a time-lapse filmed flower that blooms in reverse,
Each day brought some further cruel deforestation
Of mind, with no hope for one thought's restoration.
He'd thought that her being alive would defray
His sadness, but all this goodbye without going away
This brutal, unsightly, and cold disappearing
Was so beyond what he'd conceived ever fearing;
A stupid, but no less dispiriting coda
To be slapped by his mother, who wanted his soda.
This someone he'd loved and so viscerally known . . .
It left Josh abandoned and feeling alone.
More than his mother uncensored, unkempt,
Was the non-recognition. Her blanket contempt
Made him feel like they'd never met, wholly a foreigner,
Meriting no more regard than the plant in the corner.
This being a stranger was like being dead,
And brought to mind how, in a book he had read
That most folks misunderstood one common state:
The flip side of love is indifference, not hate.

Since Shulamit left with the kids, he had mused
On all of the ways he had sinned and abused
Those people and things in his vacuous life
He'd thought that the money he'd made for his wife
Was all that she wanted. Turns out he was wrong,
But his Augustine moment had taken too long.
It had all come as such a bright bolt from the blue,
He had no choice but to assume it was true.
 "You're empty," she'd said. "A money-drunk fool.
Neglected your soul for the sake of a *pool!*"
To add to this gumbo of guilt, there was Nathan;
Remorse was a river so deep he could bathe in.
SusanSloanShulamit told him as much:
He was venal and shallow and used as a crutch
All the trappings and nonsense, the things he had bought
    her.
She wanted the children and he hadn't fought her.
He missed them so much, his sweet girl and boys,
But he *had* to allow it, since he was the poison.

For himself, like some ex-con or monastic novice
He'd found a small studio right near his office.
It struck him as fitting, a concrete admission
Of guilt: one's apartment as form of punition.
In such a bare space, he might do some soul-healing,
With room for the boxes, stacked from floor to ceiling.
He now had the unwanted stuff of two houses,
The one of his boyhood, and all of his spouse's

Possessions. He'd store them and keep a close eye on
The boxes, in case she might ever return home from Zion.

Now here he was, fifty, and starting anew
On a path he'd attempt to keep virtuous and true.
He'd found among Sloan's many things she'd acquired
A delicate necklace of sterling barbed wire
Whose points had been rounded with small silver
        bearings
Though it still gave some punishing hurt in the
        wearing,
And wearing it daily, he was, 'round his waist,
A constant reminder to keep him abased
And not tempted by temporal glorification.
He found that he needed such mortifications.
A bed, chair, and table were all that he had
Along with the knowledge (hard-won): He was bad.
Friends understood the pained cast to his eyes,
He'd won the annus horribilis prize;
Losing his wife and bereft of his Mommy
2006 was a perfect tsunami
Of all that the Lord seemed to have in His toolkit
Of sadism, suffering, spite, pain and bullshit.

Unpack a box, then an act of contrition.
Draw one bead of blood, could the Bowery Mission
Make use of some never-worn cashmere sweaters?
(Another knife prick: *All on earth are my betters!*)

He'd come to depend on these tiny surrenders.
How does one family end up with three blenders?
Forty more sit-ups, a stone in his shoe,
Keep two suits for work, one gray and one blue.
After eight weeks, he'd grown saintly and lean
And addicted to his ascetic routine.
Until late one night he was mindlessly sorting
Sloan's shoes when a box he found brought him up short.
Just two words in marker, but two were enough
To accordion time. It was labeled, "Ted's Stuff."

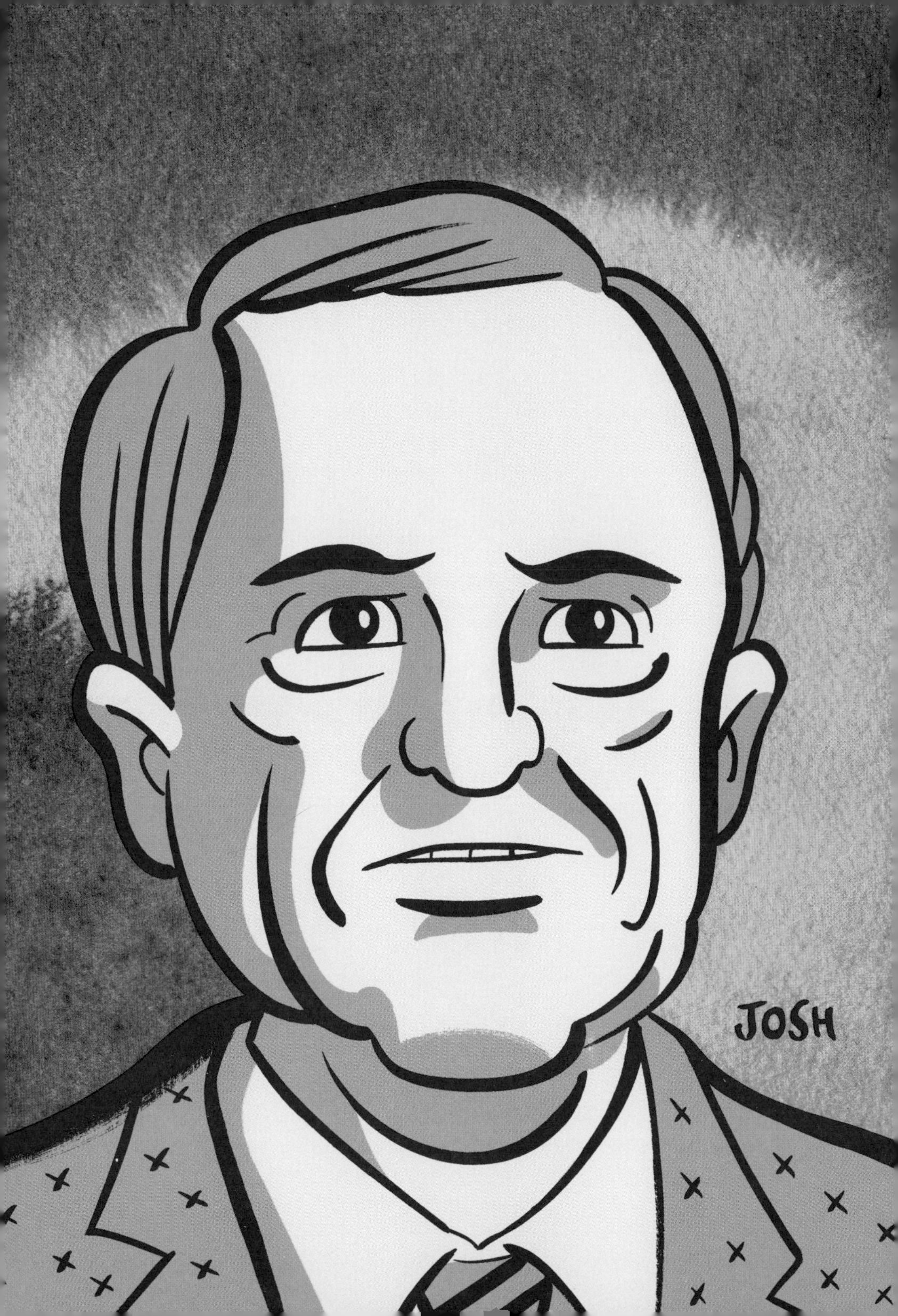
JOSH

Maybe, she thought, even this rocky tor
Was no random pile, but concealed something more
Than mere sandstone and lichen, wind-smoothed,
    sun-bleached;
Perhaps it was here where He might have once preached,
Since everywhere seemed to have some place in history,
All was laid bare and yet shrouded in mystery.
She'd heard it on late-night *shmirah*, on guard duty
Where, taking in all of the harsh desert beauty,
Starlit and bleak in the hematite dark,
The words "Son of God," followed by "Joan of Arc."

The news filled her spirit, she felt she might burst
And for a split second thought, *Who to tell first?*
'Til reason returned and she realized they'd hate her,
Label her crazy, a perjuring traitor.
Shulamit knew what they likely would say,
But naturally saw things a different way:

She'd needed to be here. No con game, no trick.
Her life was a cancer, her spirit was sick.
Her impulse in coming was out of pure love,
And a spiritual yearning to cleanse herself of
The secular world that had previously taught her

To name their girl Dylan, like Ralph Lauren's daughter.
(As redress, in part, for her *goyische* folly
Chip was now Duvid, and Schuyler, Naftali.)
The searchlights and razor wire, satellite phones
The high keening wail of the *Hagana* drones,
She'd loved it all, all the belief that it rested on
But knew in her heart that she had to be moving on.

Shulamit knew that she'd tell them all how
Each moment was whole; Then was Then, Now is Now.
Moving here, loyally calling this place her new home meant
No more and no less than it did in that moment.
The settlement would, she knew, find this appalling
But Shulamit now knew to answer each calling,
The way that a rocket ship's solid-fuel stages—
Sloughed off and discarded—she'd passed through such ages
And people to one day reach idealization;
After all, it's the journey, not the destination.

———————

"Ted's stuff." Nine letters, the moment was fixed,
A man he'd last seen alive in '66.
An integral part of existence and then
He dropped dead of a heart attack when Josh was ten.
There was no deep nerve touched, no significant metaphors
Just a few potent, outstanding sensory semaphores:
Orange juice poured from a cut-glass carafe,
Corn Flakes he drowned in some chilled half-and-half.

And swimming! It seemed he swam a million-and-two laps,
"Let all you others have spare tires and dewlaps!
You can be thought of as kindly and honest,
And I'll gladly be the local Adonis!"
Scandalized cries of "You schmuck" and "Oh, Ted."
A pitcher of something grown-up and deep red,
Laughter and drinks on a dark summer lawn,
A green shirt, a candle . . . the moment was gone.

Forty years later, the tape simply shattered
To bits. Well, the contents could hardly have mattered.
And yet, Josh's response, he'd have never dared posit
Such a strong recollection of the old front-hall closet.
He was *there* through some magical olfactory feat!
Josh's eyes briefly fluttered, his heart skipped a beat.
He would hide in there, nightly, crouched down on the
        ground,
Until Ted threw the door wide and yelled, "Ha, I have found
        you!"
And here it all was, through the strongest of spells,
That closet brought forth by the myriad smells:

The forest of coats, an old rolled-up rug
Gave off a comforting, camphorous fug.
It almost seemed noisy, the darkness so full
With the various scents wicking out of the wool.
Dust that had burned on the coils of a heater,
Cigarettes, perfume, and nights at the theater
Mothballs, pressed powder forgotten in lockets.

A half roll of Life Savers fused to the pockets,
And in yet another, a lone unwrapped mint
Had bundled itself in a stole of gray lint.
Nightly, in p.j.'s, the smells would surround
Him 'til that thrilling moment of "Ha, I have found you!"

And here, some black oxfords, irretrievably scuffed,
Some moth-eaten jackets, the pockets all stuffed
With envelopes—he counted at least thirty-two—
All scrawled with the message, "Josh, these are for you."
Inside each were handfuls of old foreign stamps.
Some of the packets addressed to the camps
He'd been sent to the summers of age seven–eight.
But what were they from? It was now far too late
For questions: Why keep them? Why weren't they just
      tossed?
From "Ha! Being found" to irrevocably lost.

He sifted his fingers through the colorful squares.
They'd been cut and assembled with obvious care.
To do this then keep them seemed such needless bother,
Unless the stamps hadn't been gifts from his father.
He was getting a headache, he hadn't intended
In joining a game that was forty years ended.
One last scan of the coats to see what else was there
When his fingers caught hold of a small, rigid square.

Manila and crisp, with a trace of old grime
At one corner, but otherwise, sealed all this time.

And written upon it, a supplicant "T."
Just one timid letter, from which Josh could see
That the script was undoubtedly feminine, tender
And clearly the stamps and this had the same sender.

He eased his small finger just under the flap.
The old glue gave way with a crisp but weak snap.
Inside, an old photo with old scalloped edges,
A girl standing, topless, by flowering hedges.
On the back, a faded almost illegible rune:
He made out, "Helen, L.A., 1954. June."
There was something so present and vivid, alive. It
Was not classic "cheesecake." More artwork, more private.
She was holding two oranges, as though she was proffering
The fruit to the viewer. Or making some offering
To . . . Josh figured some boy,
But offering not sex, at all, but simply pure joy.
It was *so* pure, in fact, without smut, without guile,
That even Josh in his monkhood could not help but smile.

There was just so much Now that the picture encapsed
In the shot, this despite more than six decades elapsed.
Both the oranges' skin and the girl's sun-stroked flesh
Seemed similarly taut and impossibly fresh.
She's standing and squinting, eyes half-closed from the sun
And laughing, delighted at what's still to come.

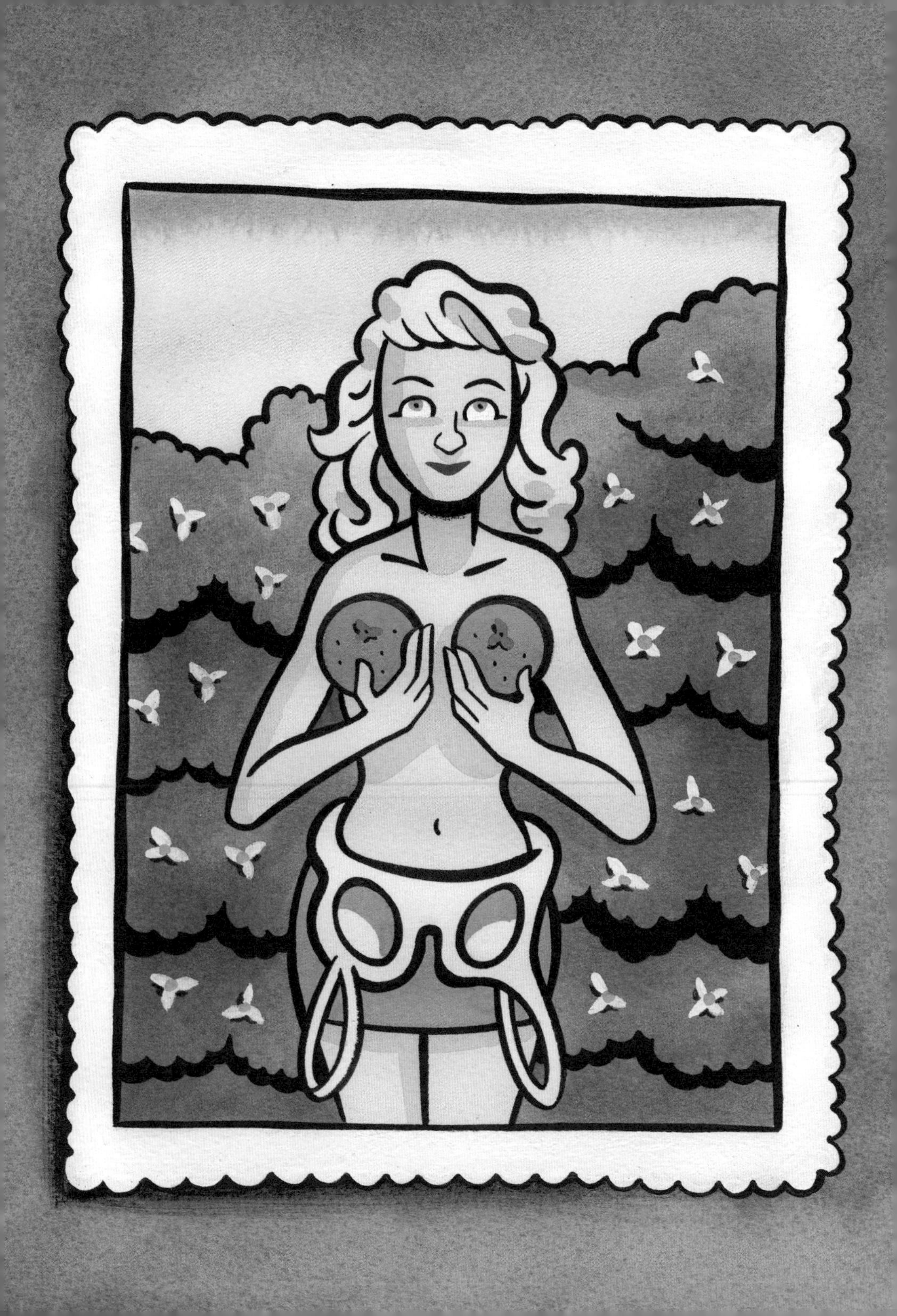

ABOUT THE AUTHOR

DAVID RAKOFF wrote the bestsellers *Fraud*, *Don't Get Too Comfortable*, and *Half Empty*. A two-time recipient of the Lambda Literary Award and a winner of the Thurber Prize for American Humor, he was a regular contributor to Public Radio International's *This American Life*. His writing frequently appeared in *The New York Times*, *Newsweek*, *Wired*, *Salon*, *GQ*, *Outside*, *Gourmet*, *Vogue*, and *Slate*, among other publications. An accomplished stage and screen actor, playwright, and screenwriter, he adapted the screenplay for and starred in Joachim Back's film *The New Tenants*, which won the 2010 Oscar for Best Short Film, Live Action. He died in August 2012 at the age of forty-seven, shortly after finishing this book.

ABOUT THE ILLUSTRATOR

SETH is the cartoonist behind the long-running comic book series *Palookaville*. His books include, *Wimbledon Green*, *George Sprott*, and *It's a Good Life If You Don't Weaken*. He is the designer for *The Complete Peanuts*, *The Portable Dorothy Parker*, and *The Collected Doug Wright*. His latest book is *The Great Northern Brotherhood of Canadian Cartoonists*, and the first of his four books with Lemony Snicket, *Who Could That Be at This Hour?*, was published in the fall of 2011.

DAVID RAKOFF
November 27, 1964–August 9, 2012

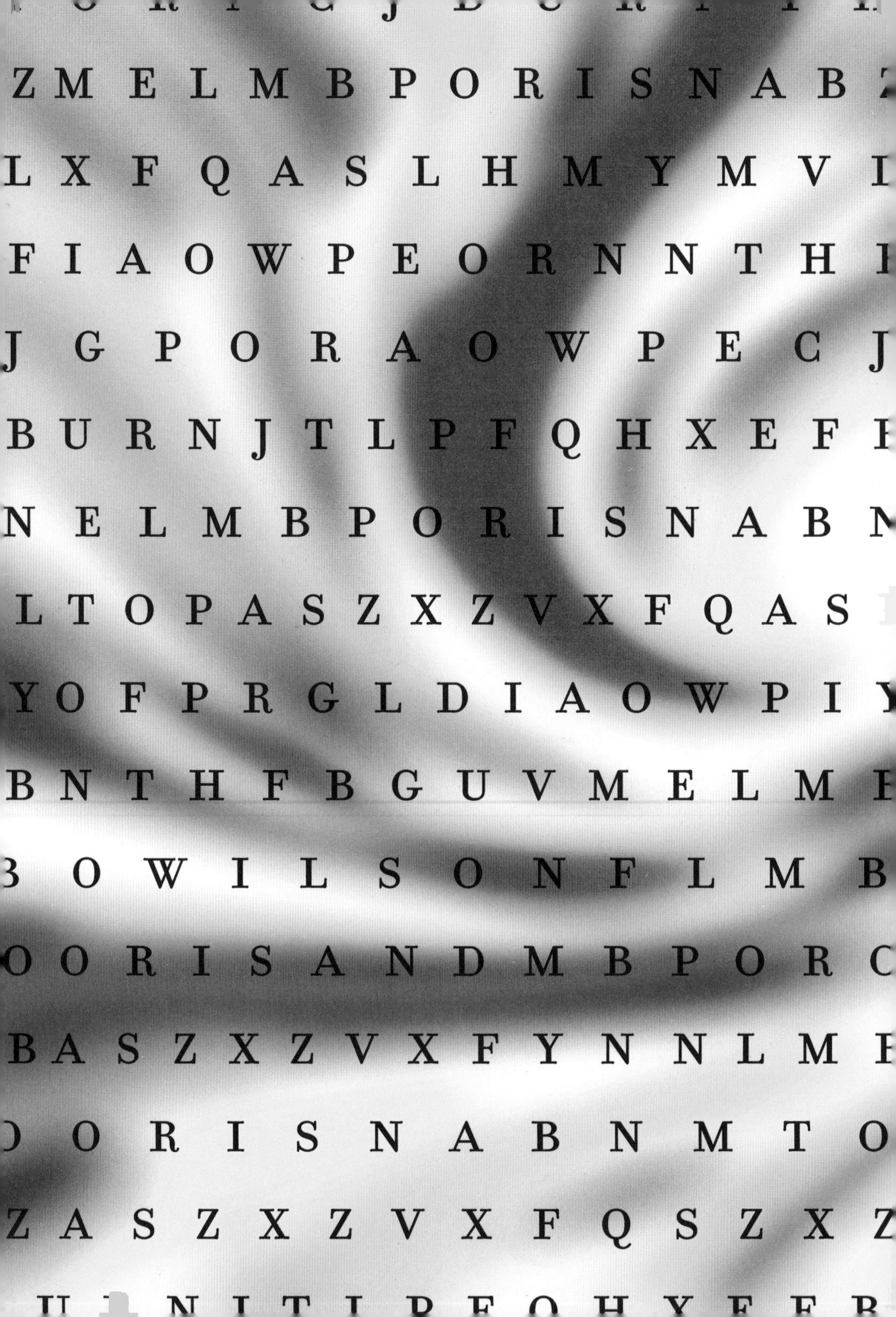
Z M E L M B P O R I S N A B
L X F Q A S L H M Y M V
F I A O W P E O R N N T H
J G P O R A O W P E C J
B U R N J T L P F Q H X E F
N E L M B P O R I S N A B
L T O P A S Z X Z V X F Q A S
Y O F P R G L D I A O W P I
B N T H F B G U V M E L M
O W I L S O N F L M B
O O R I S A N D M B P O R
B A S Z X Z V X F Y N N L M
O R I S N A B N M T O
Z A S Z X Z V X F Q S Z X Z